SNOW SHARK

Brian G. Berry

Copyright © 2022 Brian G. Berry

All rights reserved

The characters and events portrayed in this book are fictitious. Any similarity to real persons, living or dead, is coincidental and not intended by the author.

No part of this book may be reproduced, or stored in a retrieval system, or transmitted in any form or by any means, electronic, mechanical, photocopying, recording, or otherwise, without express written permission of the publisher.

ISBN-13: 9798446416981
ISBN-10: 1477123456

Cover design by: jorgeiracheta
Library of Congress Control Number: 2018675309
Printed in the United States of America

*To David Irons. Your Wolf Moon was
a huge inspiration to me.*

"You know the thing about a shark...he's got lifeless eyes, black eyes, like a doll's eye. When he comes at ya, he doesn't seem be living, until he bites ya and the black eyes roll over white."

-Quint, Jaws

CONTENTS

Title Page
Copyright
Dedication
Epigraph
Chapter 1   1
Chapter 2   12
Chapter 3   21
Chapter 4   33
Chapter 5   45
Chapter 6   55
Chapter 7   60
Chapter 8   69
Chapter 9   74
Chapter 10   84
Chapter 11   88
Chapter 12   98
Chapter 13   104

Chapter 14	116
Chapter 15	121
Chapter 16	131
Chapter 17	137
Chapter 18	142
Chapter 19	154
Chapter 20	159
Chapter 21	164
Chapter 22	170
Chapter 23	175
Chapter 24	181
Chapter 25	186
Chapter 26	196
Afterword	199

CHAPTER 1

Northern Siberia
1988
0230

At first, it wasn't much of an issue. The Polaris cut a wedge through the snow as if it were a glass lake. But once his team ditched the craft, and their boots crunched through drifts in the woods, progress had become mired with complications. But the command was adamant about discovering just what had landed in their backyard. Colonel Grisha was going mad with interest. He couldn't quite handle the fact that something pinged his radar, ghosted his systems, then a moment later made a splash somewhere out in those woods just beyond the perimeter of his post.

Sergeant Pyotr Antonov commanded a small contingent of Spetsnaz—Soviet Special Forces—that acted as a security element assigned to the outpost to counter aggression from enemy incursions that may threaten operations, and his unit was tasked with discovering just what sort of thing dropped out of orbit and buried itself in the blowing white storm.

It wasn't something he was expecting to be roused with at 0230 in the morning, but, he was Spetsnaz, proud and unwavering in the face of adversity. His men on the other hand, though loyal in their bonds and oaths, were not at all too thrilled to be gearing up for a little adventure in the cold woods at this time of night, when such a storm was throwing mountains of drift around the land, pecking at the windows with flakes too thick and plush to see much of anything out in the black and pale landscape.

After the men grieved and bitched, Pyotr harried his men to the storage building outside —the one with the big weather resilient steel retracting door sealed tight by a seam of ice.

After breaking their way inside with a torch, the men mounted their winter steeds and sped off into the night; five dots that were soon consumed over by a steady sheet of knotted flakes.

Once they hit the woodline, dismounted their craft, popped a tarp over the vehicles, and put their boots in the snow, it was dreadful. Luckily each man was insulated from the blow by his winter gear and balaclava, goggles, and fatigues that might have kept a man warm, but afforded no real maneuverability—which could spell disaster if faced with an enemy force.

Fighting the drifts, pushing through the flakes, the men instantly broke security, started moaning about the storm and all the snow it brought with it, and how there was nothing so important to rally them from such a warm bed on such a cold, black night. But sergeant Pyotr kept his resolve, reminding his men that even though it was highly unlikely for them to clash with an enemy force so far out in this frozen winter hell, they had to keep their resolve about them and act like soldiers—even as the wind blew a snowball of flakes into his goggles, plugging the barrel of his rifle with ice.

After clearing a painstaking distance of soft pack and howling high winds, the men settled into the misery. Blades of light fixed to their rifles cut through the snow, putting distance to the black that all but absorbed their forms in the blizzard.

Pushing through a wall of pines, the men disgorged from the woods to the foot of a wide clearing. Even in night, the men could see out across a vast plain of white. Flakes clogged their beams as they looked out across the pale bed of snow that stretched ahead of them in a flat frozen sea. But it was what their lights disclosed out in the center of the frosted ocean that caused the men to lock up jaws, and stare curiously. It was some sort of metallic object from the looks of it. And what drew the points of their eyes was the light on the object that beat the night away with its incessant blue pulse.

"Alright," Pyotr shouted over the wind, gathered around his men. "Follow my steps, watch your sectors—I don't know what the hell that is, but we're heading over to find out."

The men fell in line, crunching, moaning, bitching, as white flakes thick as cotton balls beat against their advance.

Clearing a good sixty to eighty meters, they spread out around the object sticking up out of the snow, leaning like some sort of landmark revealed by the blowing wind, that all that bitching and complaining went silent. Whatever it was, it was split open down the center roughly in the shape of an 'A' lacking the center dash. It stood taller than two men. There was a panel of buttons that were pale in color, and above it, a blue light that pulsed like a rapid heart about to burst.

"What the hell is that, sergeant?" One of the men, Yuri, asked. He tapped the muzzle of his AK against the skin of the object. It was hard and thick, registering a sound as a stone would make smacked with a hammer. "Hard material; strong enough to survive impact, that's for sure."

Pyotr scanned the canister but hadn't a clue as to what he was looking at. "Maybe a bomb?" he said, looking up to the sky which his eyes and light failed to penetrate.

That was foremost on all of their minds. But where was the detonation? An explosion would have been recorded back at command. Besides, bomb casings were typically reduced to molten shards on impact. This thing was whole, unblemished, though slit up the middle like something was released from its core.

"Lev, call it into Grisha," Pyotr called over his

shoulder. "He'll want a helicopter crew out here come morning to dig this out."

"Yes, sergeant."

"Anatoly—Kodiak," Pyotr called out. "Start chopping us a shelter to escape this hell while we take readings."

There was no reply, and Pyotr blamed the whistling gusts whistling in his ears. He looked up from the canister and put his light to where his men were just standing a moment ago.

"*Anatoly? Kodiak?*" He shouted over the wind and snow.

Lev swung his light around. Yuri, too, swept over the area.

"Where the hell did those two get off to?" Pyotr held his rifle out ahead of him. Its light swept the woods behind him, stabbed the dark at his flanks. He ran its blade over the snow around him now, looking for tracks, anything to indicate his men took off. He quickly pushed the notion of that absurdity out of his mind. Besides, his men would never abandon their posts without a word.

Suddenly, Yuri shouted over the wind. "Sergeant Pyotr!"

Pyotr put his light on his comrade. "What is it?" he shouted, wiping buildup off his goggles.

"I…I don't know…"

Pyotr had a bad feeling roll up in his gut. His boots fought snow as he headed over to Yuri who was stuck to the earth like some sort of lethal snowman with his rifle pointing to the ice.

Pyotr drew up beside him. "What is—"

The air went right out of him after putting his light into the snow.

"I don't know what this is," Yuri said, maybe not wanting to admit what he was seeing.

"It's blood, Yuri," Pyotr said flatly, running his light over the mess, nearly choking on the words.

Lev came shuffling up beside the two. His light added to the scene. "What—where is Kodiak? Where is Anatoly?"

Pyotr's throat and tongue went dry, his mind was working to make sense of the remains at his boots. Where his men had once stood, there was now a gaping red abyss. Not a puddle, or even a stain, but like a detonation of blood had blown a hole in the ground, splashing red in a wide halo. There was no indication of a fight, no bullet casings, no boot prints, not much of anything —just a crater of hot blood that slowly burned further down to the soil with its density and heat. Snow was hitting it in heavy flakes, concealing all that red over with a layer of white.

"We double back," Pyotr said, his voice visibly cracked and shaken, eyes on that red soup at his boots. "We bring back a search party—"

"I'm not leaving our men behind," Lev dictated, his voice loud and booming over all that wind. "Spetsnaz don't leave comrades behind—alive or dead!"

"Be sensible," Pyotr countered, his usually commanding brogue faltering with the fear inching up his throat. "We don't even know what the hell happened here!"

"Well, men just don't dissolve into piles of blood and disappear, sergeant!" Lev stammered.

As Pyotr and Lev argued over what to do, Yuri screamed. And it was a foul shrieking howl that whipped over the men with a blood-curdling agony.

Both Pyotr and Lev swung their weapons towards Yuri.

Their lights came together and what they saw caused both of the men to scream out in reply. Yuri was on his belly, his hands and fingers clawing at the snow as if he dropped into a deep hole fighting to push himself out. He was screaming and shouting, said something was biting into him, and its resonation competed with the wind.

Pyotr was locked up at the sight, but Lev dashed forward to help his comrade on elbows and knees when Yuri suddenly went rigid as a tombstone and was dragged back into the polar black across the pale sea. His screams grew in torturous agony, growing fainter in the howling winds of the storm.

"Jesus Christ!" Lev shouted, pointing his muzzle out across the white expanse. He stood, and fumbled back to Pyotr who was still locked up in the snow, shivering, but not from the cold. "WE HAVE TO GO, SERGEANT! NOW!"

Pyotr snapped back with a delayed scream, something that had built up with a terrible volume. "YURI!"

"HE'S GONE, SERGEANT!" Lev had to remind him. "We have to get out of here—back to the Polaris!"

Lev took his sergeant's arm and started tugging and dragging him back towards the woods, much like a scared child locked up after seeing something so frightful. After a few tugs and twists and shouts, Pyotr appeared to regain composure of himself and hurried behind Lev.

The snow continued its lashing assault over them both, hampering strides, frosting their goggles, dusting their rifles.

Lev was the first to reach the woods, where the snow was not as thick as what that frozen oasis put under their boots; protected mostly by the weaving high boughs of pines looming white and black overhead.

Pyotr was a shadow that stumbled forward beaten and shrouded with flakes. Lev watched him, but kept his eyes on the white sea, scanning with his weapon at whatever hidden terror lurked around the snow, or in it. Checking his flank, he called to his sergeant over the wind: "PYOTR, HURRY WE—"

There was nothing there, and his voice fell silent with dread.

Nothing to greet him but a frozen waste, and a whistling, howling wind that blew right over him and through him.

"PYOTR!" Lev cried. And it was a cry like something a child would scream abandoned by the shield of a parent in the midst of some Halloween haunt. "PYOTR!"

A snap in the brush jerked away his focus on the clearing.

His light fluttered through the woods, causing shadows to jump and grow and lean. He put his weapon on fire, anticipating some barreling monstrosity to burst forth out of the thick snow-capped pines. Something moved, he saw it, just aside the base of a large group of firs. It was vague, but he saw movement in the snow. He kept his light on the spot, thinking he would see it again. He waited, but nothing moved—nothing but flakes caught in snaking streams curling through and around stocks of pines. As he went to lower his rifle, the snow exploded in a white cloud in front of him, blowing over him with lumps and plumes of ice.

His rifle responded, cracking apart the night with its angry retort. Flames jumped from the barrel, brass hissed in the snow.

He quickly changed magazines, stared off into the woods, frightened at what he would see emerge. But there was nothing there—just more wind and snow packing over him, burying his brass, clouding his goggles, steaming on the barrel.

Breathing hard, sucking in the cold air, he fought his way through the woods, the whole time thinking something was on his trail as timbers creaked and cracked with each step he put further away from the white sea and its lurking haunter.

He would swing back now and again, but there was nothing there that would draw a bead, just a black wall of night, and flakes caught in his beam.

After reaching the snowmobiles, Lev hurried to start the motor. It coughed a few times before turning over, and he sailed off across the clearing. Two miles and he would be safe. Away from whatever horror waited in the snow. Flakes smacked his face and screened the headlight, but he didn't care. His heart was hammering like his rifle did back in the woods. He kept looking over his shoulder, but it was a useless gesture. The dark was a solid mass that he could never hope to penetrate.

Something bumped into his Polaris, and he had to tell himself that, no, you hit something, nothing bumped into you. How absurd in thinking such things!

Again, something bumped into him, and this time he had trouble convincing himself. Drooling, his teeth chattering beneath the mask, snow raking his face, sticking to his fatigues, something rammed him with the speed and strength of a logger's rig. Lev was thrown from the tiny craft and went spinning in the air a good twenty feet before crashing down into a thick drift that sucked him down to the waist.

For a moment, there was no movement, then slowly he shook his head and realized he was alone in the snow. Alone without his rifle—without his light. The sky was black as the cold space beyond the stars, the snow kept up its merciless lashing. If he didn't hurry himself up, he would be weighted down, stuck in that pack, left to freeze over into a solid block that would never thaw.

Pushing with his palms, he glimpsed something out in the snow. Even with the lack of a beam to guide his eyes, he saw it. It was there, just beneath the surface. Lev started to claw at that snow with much more force, digging his hands in and scooping his way out, moaning and crying in his throat. He was nearly free when something hurried forward. He felt it; could feel its vibrations like the aftershocks of a quake. He saw the snow bulge as if something was tunneling through it, then something breached the surface. Something narrow yet strong to cut a path like a blade through ice. Lev screamed when something big and terrible burst through the white at his hands, tossing snow in his face. A hot odor went up his nose, and he shrieked in the suffocating cavern of impossible fangs that swallowed over him, grounding his bones and body into a red paste that dragged across the snow, and was quickly obscured by the fall.

CHAPTER 2

Alex Henning was having trouble listening to his wife bitch about all that snow that hemmed the single-lane mountain road with waves of white. Listening to "I'm Never Gonna Dance Again" by George Michael was on his mind. His lips repeated word and chorus, unimpeded by her insistent nagging. The speakers were scratchy, lacking the crash of a proper bass, but Alex didn't mind. Didn't mind at all. George Michael's voice rang harmoniously in the confines of his '87 wagon. Seated in the back, his children never really cared what their daddy listened to—they enjoyed his choice in music. Unlike their mother. It was as if she were a constant note in whatever musical choice their father decided to fill their heads with.

"Alex, watch out for that corner!" she shouted over Michael's verse.

Alex retorted with lyrics, dragging his wheel to the left, mindful of where he was going even with the track raging from his speakers.

"You're going to give me a heart attack," Corrina said.

Not bothering to lend a word to that comment,

Alex continued up that white slope, tires grinding ice, flakes pecking the windshield, and his children in the back had their faces pushed against the window.

"How much further, sweetheart?" Corrina asked, easing her tone.

Alex swung the dial up on the radio; Michael's voice crashed through the speakers. He was trying like hell to drown that chattering voice cutting his ears with questions that had no real tangible answer to return.

"We'll be there when we get there, babe, I told you that. No telling how long it will take. A few more miles, but with this snow, could be another hour."

"Another hour," she shouted over the closing beats of the track. Corrina silenced the stereo. "Another hour?" she repeated as if he had somehow not heard her words.

"Yeah, maybe less—it's coming down hard."

It was. It was dumping on that little blue wagon, filling the tracks that stretched far behind its path in muddy bars, dusting the pines with heavy fall that sagged branch and buried trunk.

"What if we get stuck?" She asked, biting at her thumbnail.

"Not to worry," he said. "I got a kit put together in the back, including a shovel, we'll be good."

As Corrina continued to chisel her nail between her lips, and worry over the buildup packing on the road, Alex rolled the dial on the stereo. "Damn," he said after a moment. "Not getting anything now." Static greeted each channel. Remembering the case of cassettes beneath the passenger-side seat, he asked, "Hey babe, can you get my tapes—they're under your seat."

Corrina sat forward, her fingers poking empty space. "Nothing here, sweetheart."

Alex eased the wagon around a clump of ice. "You sure? It's in a black velcro case, should be easy to find."

Corrina once again ran her hand beneath the seat. "Not feeling anything."

"Caleb," Alex said over his shoulder, speaking to his son. "You see my cassette case back there? Under your mom's seat?"

Caleb looked, put his hand under there, but like his mother, came up empty. "Nothing dad."

"Damnit, I thought I put them under there. Megan, can you check my side, sweetheart?"

Ten-year-old Megan Henning ran her tiny pink gloved fingers under her daddy's seat, but only brushed against something hard. "Nothing, daddy," she said after a minute. "There is something hard under there."

"Nah, that's just part of the seat—the reason why I keep the case on the other side."

Frustrated with his lack of tunes, Alex put some weight on the accelerator. There was a flare in the tail end of the wagon; tires spinning without traction, the sound of ice crushed beneath the chassis.

"Alex, what are you doing?" Corrina asked,

grabbing the leather loop bolted above the door at the sudden increase in speed.

"Just trying to hurry us along. I want to reach that resort!"

"Well, driving like this won't help—you're going to get us stuck—or worse."

"I told you I have a snow kit—just in case. We'll be fine!"

"They're fighting again," Caleb Henning told his sister. "It must be a record—two hours and not a single fight."

Megan was busy dragging her fingertip on the window, carving a line through the frost glazing up the glass, unconcerned about her parents' bickering that was common enough that she had learned to silence their tantrums by going inside her head.

Caleb turned away from his sister after she offered no reply.

He put his eyes on the snow; looked up at a sky that was screened in heavy flakes, to a wall of woods no longer green with pine but curtained white and cold.

Fourteen years of age, he would be spending his birthday on this mountain—at the resort. His parents promised him a good one. Said he would have plenty of presents to put a smile on his face. It was hard to keep his eyes off that box that was bulging in multicolored paper and big looping bows. There was one particular box inside that bigger box he had his mind working on. He was hoping that rectangle wrapped in blue silk with a silver bow was the Nintendo Entertainment System. That's all he'd been hounding his mom and dad for.

Mom, dad, he'd say, all I want for my birthday is the Nintendo!

They would say, Well, that's a lot of money, Caleb, but you keep asking, and if not for your birthday, maybe Santa can help you out for Christmas.

Waiting ten months didn't sound so appealing, considering he'd been asking for a couple of years now. He just hoped that all that backlog of whining and moaning about the Nintendo would finally prove beneficial.

"What about the gear on top of the car?" Corrina asked.

"I secured it—it ain't going nowhere, babe," Alex told her. "You need to stop worrying so much, we're almost there, and then maybe you'll be able to relax in that awesome room of ours."

Before Corrina could reply, the sound of a horn drew her head to the rear window. Frosted over, seeing had become difficult, but she saw enough to understand that the big brown blob filling the window was a truck, and from the sound of it, a pissed-off driver behind the wheel.

"What the hell is this?" Alex asked, his eyes on the rearview mirror.

"Just pull over, sweetheart, let him pass if he wants to act like an idiot."

Another shout of the horn made his blood hot. "No

—he can wait like everybody else has to wait!"

"What everybody else?" Corrina said incredulously. "It's only us and our children—let me remind you. No reason to get into something with this guy."

Alex wasn't listening. He had his eyes on the truck riding his bumper and smashing its horn. It amazed him that some people could act as they did on these forest roads, so far removed from emergency services. Weren't they concerned with getting in a wreck? Who would that benefit? Ego? It mattered none because right then Alex was showing his ego, pulling more into the middle of the road, not allowing a sliver that would compel the man behind him to glimpse a passage.

"What are you doing?" Corrina demanded to know. "Alex, pull over right now—let this asshole pass!"

More shouting of that horn was all he was hearing. "Take notes kids," Alex said, his eyes on every mirror, ignoring his wife. "Never let somebody bully you!"

"What are you talking about?" his wife shouted. "Nobody is bullying anybody, he simply wants to pass—we're going too slow for him!" Seeing that look in her husband's eyes, she knew that Alex wouldn't stop. He got like that sometimes; on roads, even in public. But it was rare. But right then it was alive. She understood how fast this could accelerate. "Alex, you pull this vehicle over right now," she demanded, then added in a whisper and a glare in her eye. "Or you can forget about special time at the resort."

The truck was weaving its bulk behind the little wagon, rage in its engine, horn screaming. Alex looked to his wife, his face dropped. Faced with the prospect of not sinking himself inside his wife, he reluctantly hugged the edge of the road, and slowed his pace, coming to a rest in a berm of thick snow-dusted in mud and pine needles.

The truck pulled up and tossed a shadow over the small blue wagon. Its passenger window was inching down. Alex saw it and wondered if he should say something. It was clear the man inside was intending to let some words off his chest.

"Alex?" Corrina warned. "If you say anything, it better be an apology."

Cutting his window down, the man inside the truck let him have it.

"Boy, what the fuck is your problem? You trying to get somebody killed up here?" Two men sat inside the truck, one was young, black beanie cupping his skull, a thick winter coat sheathed his arms, a wry grin pulling at the corner of his lips; he was leaning back a space to allow the older man with a face full of brown beard and a brow twisted in anger beneath a thick blue beanie to shout out his frustration.

"You better watch yourself on these roads, boy!" The older man, name of Ray Weston, said. He glanced past Alex and put his eyes on the beauty seated next to him. "Sorry about my vicious tongue, ma'am, but your hubby there needs to learn to correct his anger, driving all wild like that."

Corrina smiled and brushed a lock of crimson out of her cream jaded eye. "Sorry, sir, I'll make sure to have a word with him."

Alex looked to his wife, had something to tell her, but forgot after that beautiful pale oval became stone. Alex looked over at the man. "I—I'm sorry, sir," he relented. "Promise it won't happen again."

Corrina took her husband's hand, rubbing a thumb over the back. "Thanks, sweetheart."

"Keep your head about you, boy," Ray Weston told Alex. "Would hate to come back down this hill, see your family crushed in some horrible accident."

Alex wanted to reach out and slap the man for the obvious, though lightly veiled threat but kept his calm instead. "You're right, sir. Again, sorry."

Ray said something else, but the young passenger cut the words off by scrolling up the window just as more verbal blades bounced inside.

Alex caught a glimpse of the truck as it pulled past. On its side, in big white block letters, it said: Ray's Septic Services.

As Alex watched the truck mulch snow and ice beneath its tires, clawing up the hill with ease, Corrina said, "Thank you, sweetheart. That was very mature of you."

"Yeah, yeah," he said, wiping flakes off his arm and securing his window.

Pulling into the snow, he tried his luck with the

radio again. "Damn, still nothing but static!"
Corrina rolled her eyes.
Megan continued her frost art on the window, oblivious to the world.
And Caleb kept hoping for that Nintendo.

CHAPTER 3

Crossing Pacific Ocean,
Entering WA Airspace

It was in the belly of that C-130 that the container sat. About fourteen feet in length, round as an oil barrel; the thing inside was crammed into a space that could hardly contain its bulk. On the outer casing was a specially engineered absorption material that would make impact of the object a success no matter the terrain or weather involved in its deployment. Thick yellow bands strapped over the casing, anchoring the object to a broad slab of plank resting on the deck, ready for immediate conveyance.

Standing at its side, a clipboard thick with notes in his hand, was Colonel Ben Heywood, scratching out some last-second readings. He reached out and poked a set of digits into the panel etched into its exterior. "All secure, vitals are stable. It's alive and ready for its next test, sir."

"Excellent," the voice on the headset said. "What of the men? I expect results were more than satisfactory?"

"Indeed, sir," Heywood remarked. "The Soviet radar installation was rendered inoperable. Those who survived the shark were dispatched by our commando element, and the information from the mainframe systems has been recorded."

"Make sure to offer my congratulations to each man involved."

"Yes, sir!"

"What is your ETA?"

"In two hours we will land at the National Guard airstrip for refueling, then we'll be wheels up and heading for DC, sir."

"Good work, Heywood," the voice said. "Secretary Conner will want a full debrief in the morning, as well myself. I expect details, Colonel."

"Yes, sir!" Said Heywood, adjusting the headset. "I have full notes and after-action reports ready to indulge."

"Capital! This could prove to be your greatest accomplishment yet, Colonel."

As Heywood chatted to the man on the headset, sergeant Darrell Trent was lost in his head. He was seated in the cargo rack attached to the bulkhead beside his team who were slumped in rest, or like himself, reflecting on that thing that was entombed in the canister at the foot of their boots. A powerfully built compact frame, a somber brow of which beneath dark eyes sat in thought, dark hair. Former Army Special Forces (Green Beret), Trent now had the responsibility of leading a small cell of operators culled from the best the military had to offer. A group with a considerable history. From testing highly sensitive and covert military technology to carrying out numerous deniable operations across the globe. Their latest venture in Siberia had taken a toll on his mind.

"Can't get over those eyes," sergeant Lynch said to himself, staring down at the canister. "Glowing like that."

Trent remembered those eyes too. Haunting red eyes that had the radiance of a lambent ruby. It was not so much the eyes that Trent ruminated over, however, but the dead. Not much was left behind, mostly just long red smears in the snow; remains mutilated by jaws and left to collect ice. He shivered at the thought of facing that thing alone; couldn't comprehend the terror each of those men must have felt as the shark came out of the snow with that wide black maw crammed with too many teeth, staring into those eyes that looked much like glass bulbs full of blood. Even with the transmitter that would disable the shark linked to the neuro-chip implanted intricately into its brain, it still brought a chill to frost his bones, thinking of the possibility of it becoming wild and uncontrolled, left to hunt men and animal in the snow, unopposed to its wrath.

Once they retrieved the shark, Trent and his men moved into the installation and did what they did best. Their weapons made quick work of the remaining personnel and troopers—most of who were caught unaware of the team's intrusion and their silent methods. Once safely inside the command structure, Trent reactivated the shark to patrol the perimeter. He caught glimpses of its dorsal cutting through the snow and saw its eyes breach the pack, luminous and terrible. After they hacked the mainframes and gathered the necessary intelligence required for their operation, Trent thumbed the button on the transmitter, effectively paralyzing the shark of its security, placing it in a passive state that would move harmlessly at their side like some old hound waiting for a signal. Though unresponsive to the men around it, to see it swimming along beside them did nothing to alleviate deep-rooted fears of the maneater beneath the waves of dark, cold seas.

Shortly after the containment of the shark, Trent and his team had found themselves in the unfortunate position of waiting out in that whipping white climate for extraction. Contracted to make the pick-up was a Soviet pilot whose pockets bulged with American currency. Shortly after the recovery, the team found themselves inbound on a short hop to Kadena Airbase in Japan, where soon they were airborne, 35,000 feet above the blue chop of the pacific, heading east, back to the mainland.

It was only a few short hours now before the men could get away from that thing and its metal coffin. But the images of those butchered in its path; all that blood that stained the snow red, that was something that would surely spring up in the dreams of each for a long, long time to come.

"Colonel Heywood, sir," said the voice of the pilot loud and scratchy over the speaker system. "We're running into some interference with avionics, might want to check this out, sir."

Heywood finished scratching a last-second detail on the clipboard before his boots clacked the deck, receding with each step toward the cockpit in a series of thinning echoes. The men who were awoken suddenly by the pilot's digital call rubbed their eyes and stretched limbs. After a round of groans and yawns, one of the soldiers, sergeant Eddie Webber, got a look at the canister.

"Shit, we're still here with that thing?"

"Better up here with it contained, than back in those woods with it alive and mean," said Sergeant Bryan Lynch whose youth was showing in the fear that etched up his throat, that sat in his eyes. A man who lacked the experience that each soldier brought to the team, but carried his weight in courage and ambition. Tall, slender, short blond bristles hacked close to the scalp, blue eyes. Lynch proved his effectiveness as a special forces soldier hunting Marxist guerrillas in Nicaragua as part of a combined CIA/SF effort. His name soon found the lap of Trent, whose team recently lost a man during a classified operation involving robotic war-fighter technology in the jungles of Honduras. The men struggled with his addition initially, but eventually, he was accepted, however lightly his inclusion.

"I suppose so," Webber said, running a hand up the bristles of his dark face, thumbing sleep out of his eye. A capable soldier with over twenty years in special forces. His monikers varied, but most that were a curve in his small circle referred to him as Brick. Ridged with muscle, Webber was a hulking nightmare to the enemy. Dark-skinned, with eyes of chipped flint, bald, the man was an abomination of strength and cords. Years before, he had beat a man to death with a fist that was balled and strong as an iron mallet after the man refused to reveal the location of a POW camp harboring American soldiers in Cambodia. "Still, can't get those sounds out of my mind," he said. "Those men back there, screaming like that."

"Was pretty fuckin' horrible," Sergeant Shane Baxter agreed. "No way for a soldier to die —eaten alive for Christ's sake." Baxter was the silent type. Not so much in the mouth, but in skill. An artisan in the craft of man hunting and extermination. Instrumental in the teams numerous assassinations that were carried out over the years. A man whose eyes were portals of fathomless green, dark hair nearly always concealed beneath a rag of olive green or jet black. Baxter was a man whose military history was clouded with bold lines that shaded out most of the details pertaining to his record. Most were only aware of his short history working with SOG and Project Delta back in Vietnam, not much else.

"Don't make any sense," Lynch said more to

himself than anyone else. "Why make such a thing? Why invest money into something like this? Must have cost more than a battleship."

"Money is no issue to these people," Webber told him, referring to the defense department. "Imagine what else they have in those laboratories that they refuse to show the public? What sorts of projects those madmen have on the table—in production."

Trent had to wonder that himself. As his men exchanged ideas on likely—or possible—experiments taking place behind the curtain—like kids arguing over such trivial things as action heroes and comic books—Trent reflected on Siberia. Back to where those men—those Spetsnaz —were dragged into the snow, crushed by teeth bigger than a man's hand. It was one man in particular that he watched through the lens of a starlight scope. In a field of luminous jade, he saw that shark drag the man a good hundred meters before it chopped his body down into a steaming hot pile. Trent could still see the flaring black strokes of blood with each clamp of its jaw, see the man claw desperately at the flakes hammering down on his screams, all of it captured in the ocular lens. It brought a shiver to spread between his shoulders.

"Are you crazy?" Webber asked Lynch, bringing Trent out of his mind, back from Siberia. "A jelly that expands with human consumption? What good would that do? How would you stop such a thing from spreading its weight across the world? It would swallow up oceans, hell, maybe the planet!"

"I did mention that it would have a limit to its growth; some type of enzyme that would break itself down during its feeding, curbing its increase. Because without it, you just look—"

"Man, you have no idea what you're talking about," Webber laughed. "Leave the science to the eggheads, focus on that rifle in your lap."

"Wonder why they chose a shark?" Baxter asked. He had remained quiet as Webber and Lynch went back and forth with their lunatic ideas breeding in labs. But looking at that shark, he had to wonder what sort of lunatics were working in those labs.

"Because it's the perfect maneater, my friend," Webber told him. "Unless they're in the process of resurrecting a T-Rex, altering its biology with cybernetics, what better thing to spread fear into the enemy? Think of all the places we fight; all the regions our enemies occupy. Imagine knowing all that snow surrounding you and your men could harbor such nightmares. Sure would change the face of winter warfare, that's for damn sure."

"But they're only effective in the snow? Right?" Baxter wanted to know.

Webber nodded. "Nah, I heard Heywood saying it could go in water, just not salt, for some odd reason. Not sure why—makes no sense. But I suppose none of it really does."

"So lakes? Rivers, creeks? Shit like that? Freshwater?" Baxter inquired.

"Yeah, puddles, too—hey, maybe those science folks will figure out a way to have them swimming through the rain. Imagine that? Looking up in the sky, seeing a million sharks streaking down in between all that rain; maybe riding bolts of lightning," Webber laughed.

"That's ridiculous," Lynch laughed in his throat. "How are they gonna fly?"

"You know what's ridiculous?" Trent asked. All three faces turned to him. "You men sitting there arguing over speculation. If I see a shark jump out of the snow and bite a man in half, I'm thinking there is no limit to what those men at DARPA are capable of. As a team, we've witnessed some brutal creations, most lacking the depth and lethality of their creator's vision, but not this one. Heywood got it right, and I'm not so sure that's a good thing."

A sudden bank of red lights blinked overhead, throwing a scarlet aspect down the interior, onto faces. Turbulence shook the walls. Hydraulic systems engaged, hissing and shrieking. At the rear of the aircraft, the ramp slowly descended, allowing a gush of cold wind to sweep its bite into the craft. The team started shouting and moaning, grabbing hold of things bolted so a bit of turbulence wouldn't shake them loose, suck them out that increasing breach in the rear.

"What the fuck is going on?" Webber's voice competed with the wind. "Whose lowering the fuckin' ramp?"

Trent saw this as bad—real bad. Saw the locks placed at the conveyor system unsecured to the container bed which sat loosely on the rack of ball wheels. "SECURE THOSE LOCKS!"

Lynch was on his boots, following Webber and Baxter. The three moved unsteadily as the aircraft jerked as if shaken by a fist. Trent released hold of the bulkhead, took a step, but was thrown back against the webbing rack after another violent tremor shuddered through the craft.

With the ramp now fully opened, exposed to the blowing cold and wind, the men struggled to bind the locks to the deck, doing their utmost to avert a terrible disaster.

"I got one!" shouted Baxter over the roar.

"Two down!" Webber added.

Trent found his feet and dashed over to secure a third when Lynch cried out. "Three down!"

That left one. Fighting the wind which blew into him, wrapping around his arms and legs, he took a knee and felt Webber leaning over him. Both their hands clutched at the lock.

"Get that ramp up!" Trent shouted over his shoulder.

Lynch hurried himself over to the panel and hit the ramp button. It began a slow ascent, struggling to climb as the wind blew around the interior, agitating things loose, tossing odds and scraps down the length of the aircraft.

"I'm losing it!" Webber said, the knuckles on his

thick dark fingers paling with stress.

A heavy shudder shook both the men loose, tossing them back into a web of orange cargo nets with a grunt and tangled limbs.

Lynch fell forward, away from the panel, cracking his chin on the deck. Baxter hurried to his aid, helping him to stand.

"THE RAMP!" Trent's voice battled the wind and turbulence shivering through the craft.

Freeing himself from the binding bands of the cargo net, Webber pulled himself forward on knee and elbow, crawling to the canister. Cords stood out on his arms, in his neck, as he cut through the wind and forced the lock. A satisfying metal snap caused a grin and a sigh. "FOURTH LOCK DOWN!"

Trent smiled, but it was brief. Something happened. Call it an aberration of climatology, or mother nature angry with the toxic pollutants streaming from the aircraft, because some exotic force worked its way inside the metal belly like a wrathful spirit, put its fingers on the canister, and with minimal effort, jerked it from beneath those straps out into the cold white sky where it became a black dot as it plunged into the pale mountain range below.

"THE SHARK!" It was Heywood. He was standing there staring at the gaping wide white aperture past the ramp. He had the look of one suddenly struck with illness. Wasn't long before his stomach squeezed itself up his throat. His knees shook; each step forward down that aircraft was much like being pushed to your doom—head forced down on the guillotine block.

"Oh fuck," Webber said, his jaw slack. "Fuck!"

Trent could only stare as the ramp seemed to find power and slowly began to incline and seal away the cold blowing through the aircraft.

Baxter and Lynch stood silent, a look of concern clouding each of their eyes.

Heywood sat down at the plank board, bands of yellow straps piled in loose coils. He grabbed one, held it in his hands, feeling the weight of it and looked back at the ramp, now secure in its housing. A grim and awful silence hung in the cold interior.

"Somebody get me the General—NOW!"

CHAPTER 4

"Benny, get that goddamn thing in there and stop messing around, I want to get this rig down the hill before the goddamn snow buries us alive up here." Ray Weston struck a match off his thumb and put the flame to the packed end of the Pall Mall. He drew a lungful, and let it blow down his nose, smoke settled into the curls of his black beard.

"I almost got it, Wes', give me a damn moment!" Benny called out from the restroom facility.

"A moment is all we got, son, I ain't liking the looks of that sky up yonder. Hurry with it now!" Ray pulled the ember down the tube, burning a line of tobacco into a gray curl. He put a thickly gloved hand over his eyes, shielding the flakes pecking his face. "Weatherman must have forgotten to mention this goddamn storm. I reckon that's what's hitting from the looks of it."

After a good battle, Benny finished sinking the nozzle end into the toilet bowl. "Got it!" he shouted. "Hit the switch!"

"Bout goddamn time," Ray said, throwing the

lever on the vacuum. The tank came alive, the hose began to shudder as a volume of excrement and piss began to fill the narrow ribbed passage. Bold black shapes struggled up the hose, pushed along with bubbling yellow rivers and clods of paper.

Benny came stumbling outside the lavatory, shaking his gloved fingers. Snow fell on him, spotting his black beanie with ice, sticking to the fibers of his winter coat. "Got piss on me!"

Ray laughed, took another long drag, and blew it out. "Ain't the first time, son. Won't be the last."

Benny put his eyes on the sky, flakes pierced on his lashes. "Damn, it's really coming down!"

"That's what I've been telling you," Ray said, tossing the butt into the snow at his side. He looked out over the white pines buried up past the trunks with snow, ringing the backside of the lavatory building—one of three they were contracted to empty by the proprietors of White Cap Lodge. "I'm thinkin' we'll come back another day when it clears up a bit before we hit the other two," he said, not relishing the thought of puttering these back roads with snow falling in such volume.

"Reckon that's a smart thing to be doing," Benny agreed, looking out across the mounting layer of snow packing over the clearing that once looked more like a parking lot, but now resembled a good-sized pond.

"Got an extra smoke on you?" he asked.

Ray padded the front pocket on his grimy

gray Carhartt heavy coat, slipped a finger inside, grabbed the pack, and tossed it to Benny. "Matchbook inside."

Striking a flame, Benny pulled on the smoke and tossed the match. "Think we'll be good going down the hill with this load?"

"Shouldn't be a concern," Ray told him. "We've had worse."

"Suppose so." Benny took a drag. "Get a good look at that gal in the wagon?"

Ray checked the valve seals for leaks, any sort of breach that would spell disaster. "What about her?" he said over his shoulder.

"Those titties," Benny said, licking at his lips, pulling on his smoke, a vivid image of the maple-colored woolen sweater that enhanced those breasts beneath. "Wish I could have seen them without that sweater coverin' em up like that."

"Gal was blessed by the lord, that's for damn sure. Ain't nothing compared to red-headed titties, son," Ray told him.

"Lucky bastard gets to bury his face in those fun bags while I'm hauling shit and piss down a mountain of ice and snow—with your old ass on top of things."

"What you think?" Ray said, working his beanie to a more comfortable spot, the sound of the vacuum tank sucking shit and piss into its belly at his backside. "She gonna' give it up to you if you weren't busy hauling waste?"

Benny laughed, pulling from his smoke. "Maybe

if I showed her what she's missing she might just go ahead and forget about that hubby of hers—get herself a real man—a real slab of meat to play with."

"You a damn fool, boy—ain't no woman like that want to mess with the likes of you."

"Why the hell not? What's the matter with the likes of me anyhow?"

"Because boy, one: your pecker ain't nothing worthy of description, and two: well, boy, you just ugly as sin," Ray laughed, a laugh that carried into the sky, echoing through the lot.

"Yeah, fuck you, too," Benny bit back, coaling his smoke in the snow. He started to speak his mind on the insult, maybe come back with some creative words of his own, but something above, in that pewter-streaked sky started screaming. Not like a person or even an animal, but something else.

"You hear that?" Ray asked before Benny. He killed the tank, shutting down the pump and all its racket.

Benny nodded. Took a moment to speak. "I'm hearing something... But with this snow," he said, narrowing his eyes to the flakes and ice flicking against his brow, "I ain't seeing shit."

Ray put a finger to his lips as he was trying his best to get his ears to work. "Listen."

It was shrill and piercing; a distinct whistling cracked open the sky, then before their eyes could show them shape and revelation, the crashing of timber, branch, and snow, reverberated through the soles of their boots as some heavy object beyond the lavatory building, inclined up a gradient of pine and snow and brush, shook the mountain with its impact.

"What in the good loving Christ was that!" Benny shouted as a natural silence followed. "Sounded like a damn bomb fell out of the sky!"

Ray nearly pissed himself the moment those woods exploded with a deafening crack; revived a memory in his old mind—back to them days of his youth. Back when bullets were fired at him with anger; back when artillery screens fell on the men, reducing them to red craters. "Sure did, boy, sure damn did if I'm honest about it."

"Sounded close," Benny stated, boots crunching forward as if he were prepared to check on things. "Just up that incline."

"Too close," Ray countered. "I ain't liking this —let us get that hose and get off this hill. Ain't no reason for us to stick around and investigate things that have no concern to us."

"Could be a plane crash, maybe a helicopter," Benny suggested, tugging at the neck of his coat, considering going on into those woods.

"A plane crash? Helicopter? You sick in the head, boy? Ain't no plane crash—the whole mountain would have been in flames. Where's your head?"

"Suppose that's truth."

"Enough flapping—get that hose," Ray told him.

"What you so worked up about, Wes', I say something about your wife?"

"Boy, I'm not speculatin' on what dropped out of that sky, but I've been in war before you were a sticky white trail up your mommas' cooz. Whatever crashed yonder had the same whine as that Korean artillery streaking down on us back on Bloody Ridge. Besides, I'm considering it a sign to get the hell off this mountain."

Benny laughed in his throat. "You think a bomb dropped on this hill? That it? That those Russian boys had enough of Regan and his mouth, decided to get back at 'im? Drop a bomb in this little hole of a mountain town?"

"Just get that goddamn hose, boy, enough chatter. Snows' pickin' up."

Benny put his hands up, palms out. "Oh yes, sir, Mr. Ray Weston—badass septic tank hauler. Didn't think much frightened you old boy."

"Ain't nothing more frightening than being shelled, boy, you remember that when your dumbass is pressed into the next world war," Ray said, helping himself into the cab of his truck, swinging the door behind him.

"So I guess I have to do everything?" Benny shouted, waving his hands in the air, snow smacking at him. But Ray wasn't listening.

Grabbing hold of the hose, Benny jerked the length out of the toilet bowl until the nozzle mouth coughed out a clot of shit and soiled paper and piss that clumped over the seat and splashed the cinder block wall and floor with filth. Using the crank, he dragged its length through the snow, and more piss and shit leaked from its interior, leaving a runny brown yellow slash across the white lot. Securing the hose with a clamp, Benny checked the valves, when something behind him shifted in the snow.

He turned.

Saw nothing but flakes thick as cotton down covering up that brown trail, stacking the tin roof of the lavatory outbuilding, weighing pines, and frosting his shoulders.

Shrugging, he started through the soft pack clinging to his ankles, when something, again, moved out in the woods behind the lavatory.

"The fuck is that?" he said, spinning to face the white-capped pines drawn behind the facility, squinting past a sheet of thick white balls obscuring the woods in pale bars. "Probably a fuckin' bear with my luck," he whispered to himself.

Not concerning himself with investigating, he pulled open the door. A gust of snow sucked inside.

"Close that door, Goddamnit!" Ray demanded.

Leaning outside the door a ways, Benny kept his focus on that structure. "Something keeps making all sorts of noise by the bathroom."

"What the hell you talking about?" Ray asked, more concerned with the powder blowing inside the cab than with Ray's curiosity keeping half his body poised outside the truck.

But Benny kept his mouth shut, instead had his ears open to that sound. It had the same punch as boots crunching hard pack. "Maybe somebody out there?" he suggested.

"The hell is somebody doing out here in this shit?" Ray asked, agitated as he worked the heat panel on the dashboard that had decided that today it just wasn't going to work all that good.

"I dunno, Wes', just suspicious is all."

"Enough of this shit! Close that Goddamn door or you stay here with whatever the hell has your attention!"

Benny pulled his eyes off the lavatory and started to seat himself inside, but instead, he screamed. Screamed with terrible anguish charged behind it as something sharp as flamed dagger blades sank into his thigh, tearing his leg from its socket in an explosive geyser of blood.

"MOTHER MARY OF THE GOOD LORD!" Ray shouted at the sight of all that blood blowing from Benny's leg like a high-pressure hose left to run wild.

Benny had his hands down on his thigh, fingers bunched over the hole too big to properly staunch. Blood fanned between his fingers as his pulse raced with shock. His face went pale as ice at the grim sight of his blood, bright and red, flaring in crimson strokes from the crater of cracked and splintered bone and severed arteries that writhed like worms unearthed by the sun.

"OH GOD, RAY! MY LEG, RAY! MY GODDAMN LEG!"

Ray had seen men mutilated in war, but the

image was nothing easily pushed aside; nothing no amount of desensitization could prepare your mind to accept. Blood was pumping out Benny's thigh at a volume he had never witnessed in his life, and Benny was communicating that fact by screaming as high and scratchy a voice as he'd ever heard in a man in pain.

Quickly, Ray checked the cab for something to pinch the flow. He found a stash of old shop rags crammed under his seat. Jumping from the cab, his boots crunched snow as he came around the truck, moaning in his throat the whole time. Benny was paling, screaming as Ray filled the passenger frame.

"I got something here, Benny, I'ma' fix you up, okay?"

Ray balled up those grimy rags and plugged them in that hole that was too damn big. Instantly, the nest of fabric had become a black, wet bundle, soaked through with blood and bits of tissue.

"Hold pressure, Benny, hold pressure Goddamnit!"

Benny had his hands down there, but with all that blood gushing from his thigh, whatever strength he had in reserve must have been going with it, because his fingers were limp, wet, and painted red—useless to bar such a tremendous pour streaming from the gaping hollow.

Ray had to wonder just what in the hell happened but figured it mattered little at that point. What mattered was getting Benny down that Goddamn hill; into the arms of a doctor, a surgeon, something.

"Don't worry, buddy, we'll get you down this hill, you hear me? You stick with me, buddy." Down at his boots, blood soaked the white a dark crimson that steamed against the ice. Working to push Benny further into the truck to get that door secure, something crunched the snow behind him.

Ray turned and fought to glimpse past the fall that blurred his faltering ability to see. Age and bad sight had offered no help in his attempts. Endless white flakes thick and round as silver dollar coins continued to add to the increasing pack rising off the ground.

Ignoring that little voice in his head telling him something was playing out in the snow, Ray turned back to Benny, and saw the ashen complexion spilling down his face; the glazed and distant look clouding his eyes. "Hold fast now, Benny! I'm gettin' us outta' here!"

Ray went to shut the door when something behind him agitated the snow.

Ray turned, and saw something like a thick blade, but curved back, pale as a bone, cutting towards him. He would have screamed if his throat hadn't been so dry. Instead, he hurried to shut that door, but found with all the blood wet on his gloves, that his fingers were sliding and slipping over the metal of the truck as slick as they were dipped in oil.

After a few more rushed attempts at the door,

something broke the surface, splashing the truck with a cloud of ice crystals.

Ray screamed in Benny's weakening face as something hot buried itself into his waist. Bones cracked to brittle chips in his backside as his legs were separated from his body in yawning red ribbons tethered to his waist. Blood dumped, loops of intestines uncoiled, lumps of meat hit the snow, emptying Ray of all those vital things he would need to continue living a good life. Instead, each piece sank into the snow, heat coming off the pile as blood poured over all that meat.

Ray had become a writhing, mad torso, fighting to clutch onto Benny who had become catatonic and near death at the sight of Ray looking more and more like something that crawled out of the grave, craving that meaty pink lump inside his skull.

Call it an effort in benevolence, Benny reached out to Ray but lacked the strength required to contort his fingers properly. All he could do now was watch on in eyes that could no longer shift or close. Something white, nearly concealed by the streaks of snow balling on Ray's beanie, tossed a pale shadow over Benny.

In his last moments of life that beaded from his thigh, Benny saw. He saw the horror in the snow. He witnessed the broad conical nose, the mouth fall open, and its teeth, spattered red in blood, thick and sheathed in gums of pink as the jaw clamped and pulped what was left of Ray into a masticated mound of meat and broken bones.

Benny was no more a man as a statue left to gather decay; a solid slate representation of a man captured in a state of unremitting paralysis. Unable to fight, unable to free himself from the image of the thing in the snow, grinding his friend of many years into a bloody paste, he reached forward with a reservoir of strength that drove out a discharge of blood to squirt from his purple thigh. He screamed, and on the tail of that scream was his last vocalization of help and agony before the thing in the snow leaped into the cab, clamped its jaw around his body, and jerked him from the seat, dragging him into the cold waste of the parking lot, where he was broken down and juiced into a smear beneath the eyes of flaming red jewels.

CHAPTER 5

It took a moment to push his wagon up that hill, but eventually, it crested the mountain which had given its tires and engine a terrible strain; traction that had difficulty treading summer asphalt in the city had found no help in clawing and spinning ice beneath its balding tread. But it was the moment the family had eyes on the lodge that all apprehension and panic had relieved itself of their chest.

It was a great structure of cedar logs stacked with the care and perfection of a lumber king and his army of carpenters. A mighty craft that had taken years of woodwork and absolute care to detail to project such an image to capture the awe of its guests. It was a painting on a canvas; the storybook image of a great winter lodge amidst a forest of snow-sagging pines and interlocking sawtooth mountain ridges beyond its cedar spire. Not a sleepy resort of some unreached goal, but a place prosperous and swollen with guests from various classes and backgrounds. No matter the difficulty of ascending the hill it rested atop, people came to enjoy the slopes, to enjoy its pubs and eateries that clustered on its ground floor, hemmed by a plethora of souvenir booths ready to pack bags and drain banks.

Parking was manageable as most of the lot had been scraped clear of snow. A plow looped the blacktop to counter the fall that dumped from a sky more umbral than gray, imprisoning a sun behind its metal shield. In its continuous loop of the lot, salt fanned behind the rig, to further combat the pour and its glazing effect on the paving.

Slotting the wagon into a space, Alex released the belt over his chest, threw open the door, and embraced the snow and its consistent flow that bled a wall of white to shroud the ground at his boots and veil the beauty of White Cap Lodge and the snow heavy peaks.

"It's perfect," Corrina said, stepping beside Alex, marveling at the design which had the shape of a 'V' opened wide, or arms spread in embrace.

Alex had been caught unaware of his wife shouldering next to him, transfixed as he was on the structure. He turned to look into the green sparks of her eyes. He took her in his arms, a smile on his face, and crushed her with a hug. "It is magnificent. Better than the guys back at work described it, even."

Caleb came running up, boots clacking and crunching salt. "Dad, this is awesome!" He put his finger an on object rising from where the roof formed a peak. "What's that right there?"

Alex followed his son's finger. "Oh—I dunno," he said, glimpsing a narrow needle-like spike thrust from the blanket of snow heavy on the roof. "Some sort of weather-vane maybe. Almost looks like a ski sculpture or something, I can't tell this far out."

Streaming into the lodge as white dots beat their skulls and pecked their jackets and skis, were a group of vacationers in a line of bright-colored winter outfits, clustered near the entrance. Some were laughing and pulling from paper cups steaming with black offered by a roving staff braving the fall and cold to bring instant warmth to their guests entering the lodge. Others rubbed their palms and elbows, adjusting gear and scarfs lynching throats.

"So awesome, Caleb. You're going to remember this birthday! Get your sister out here."

"Megan," Caleb shouted, leaving his parent's side.

"You said our room overlooks the slopes?" Corrina asked, warming her shoulders with bright mint-colored gloves.

"Sure does—supposed to give us a great view of the lake down behind there, too. Let's hope this sky clears a bit so we can see the moon tonight."

"Oh, I bet it would be beautiful, Alex." She batted her lashes and lowered her voice in a sensual clip. "I can imagine the moon—the kids asleep—just you and me—alone, maybe in the tub?"

"Ah, you remembered the hot tub included in the room?"

She smiled, leaning in to lick his ear. "I won't be wearing anything."

Alex smiled back. "I can't wait for tonight!"

"Dad, should I grab the box?" Caleb asked, referring to the presents.

"Sure—but be careful, there are breakables in there!"

"I will, I will…" Caleb swung open the back, grabbed the box tight in his arms, and held it close to his chest.

"You sure got that, son?" Alex asked him after seeing how his arms struggled to contain the giant box. "I know it's pretty heavy."

Caleb made a face, shifting the weight off his bicep. "I got it, I got it."

After arms were loaded and heavy with gear and luggage, the car secured behind them, the four moved slow and uneasily under the added weight to the lodge. Inside, they were greeted with a gush of warm wind that thawed out any kinks in the joints and brought smiles and gasps of relief.

"Oh, so warm," Alex said, stamping his boots on a thick black mat stained with salt crumbs just past the swinging doors left to fall back into the frames by the doorkeeper. "Thank you," Alex said to the man, who then nodded.

"Wow, this place is much bigger on the inside," Corrina added to the already shocked expressions of her family.

The place was cavernous. Thronged by a hundred people clad in colorful and bright garments of all ages and sizes. A smell of damp gear permeated the air, on top of which hung a sweet pall of grilled meats and chopped dishes combined with the clanking of glass over gracious laughter and muffled conversation.

"There must be a dozen restaurants in here," Alex said, his nostrils pulling in the myriad smells sailing through the grand room. And it was a grand room, spread beneath their boots with a crimson carpet spotted in hand-sewn pine designs centered in tiny diamonds that seemed to file endlessly throughout the open chamber. The walls were cluttered with various oil paintings bracketed in grand gilt frames. Racks of skis and poles ran up the walls and sat securely in corners. Relics and shrines to famous skiers immortalized sections of the interior which saw many visitors flashing bulbs of photos, capturing these memorials to glimpse in future sittings with dusty scrapbooks.

"I can't wait to see our room!" Caleb shouted, not bothering to conceal that smile on his face, thinking of all those presents.

Alex smiled and laughed in his throat. "Rooms," he corrected. "Your sister and you will be sharing a room adjoined to us."

"You mean—"

Alex cut his son off. "That's right, your own room—but, that does not mean you guys will be unsupervised."

"But, our own room?" Caleb said, already

picturing himself playing a Nintendo console, not worried about time limits and such. "There is a television in this room, right dad?"

Alex nodded. "Yep. Nineteen-inch."

"Megan, you hear this?" Caleb asked her, but her attention was on the shop whose long stretching windows showed baskets of sweets and candies, the name above stenciled in old English: Kandy.

"Huh?" She said, all ten years of age focused on the gleaming barrels bulging with candy and rows of chocolates under a rolling glass cover.

"Our own room!" Caleb said again.

"But, I don't want our own room," she said sadly, looking at her mom.

Corrina kneeled. "It'll be okay, sweetheart, we're right next door, like our own home—just a door away. You'll be safe—Caleb will be there to protect you, too!"

Megan smiled. "Okay."

The family moved together across the space between the entrance and lobby. A man came forward, a brass cart on wheels behind him. "Can I help you with your luggage, sir?"

Alex turned to appraise the man. He was short and outfitted in red velvet slacks and top, threaded with gold stripes on cuffs, polished black shoes winked off the elk and buck chandeliers that strung over the expansive ceiling.

"Yes, please—that would be great."

After piling on their gear, the man followed at a quiet distance.

"Morning," Alex said to the man behind the counter garbed in similar wear to the bellhop waiting patiently behind them.

"Morning sir, welcome to White Cap Lodge, how may I assist you?" The chipper voice asked.

"I'm checking in. Henning—Alex Henning."

The man smacked a few keys on the computer, his chalk-white face hit green with the monitor's glow. "Yes, I have an Alex Henning with Corrina Henning, and Caleb and Megan Henning," he said, smiling down at the kids; a great big smile the kids failed to return, instead shrinking back behind their parents at the bizarre grin.

"Yep—that's us."

"Excellent," the man, plastic name-tag of Chris, said. "I'm assuming you and your family are hitting the slopes during your stay with us?"

"Oh yes," Alex confirmed. "We'll be hitting it often, you can be certain of that."

"Excellent! We have the best slopes in the state, sir," the man said, his grin wide and terrible to a child's imagination.

"That's what I've heard," Alex said, looking at his wife with a wry sort of gleam in his eyes; a hint that the man behind the counter was a strange sort with a curious twist to his voice.

"Your room—"

"Rooms," Caleb interrupted the man.

"Yes, sorry about—is it, Caleb?"

"Yeah."

"My apologies, young sir. Rooms, both come

with access to the lift free of charge—no extra cost. Also, ski rental and accessories are 40% off for our guests, so please make sure to browse the store just over there," he pointed with a pen. "You may find some equipment that would be a great addition to your gear."

Alex looked over his shoulder. "Will do, thank you."

"Now, is there anything else I can do before you and your family head up to the rooms to drop off your—"

The man paused after seeing the box bulging with presents. "And whose birthday might it be?" he asked, his brow lifted, his eyes wide and menacing toward the two children.

Caleb raised his hand, though felt some strange impulse to avoid doing so. "Mine."

"Oh, well: Happy Birthday, young lad. I hope it is enjoyable. And how old will you be turning this year?"

"Fourteen."

"A fun age," the man said, reaching beneath the counter, a gesture that at first was mistaken for a debased fumbling. "Take this. It will get you special birthday privileges during your stay."

Caleb reached for the small coupon-like packet offered to him. "Uh, thanks, I guess."

"My pleasure, young Henning."

Corrina shifted her feet. "Curious about the snowfall, is it supposed to be falling so heavy? Local news back home said the resort should be light over the next week."

The man tore his eyes away from the boy. "Oh," he said. "It happens often up here—freak storms, excessive accumulation, but it never hampers fun on the slopes, that I can assure you!"

She smiled uneasily. "Okay… thank you."

"Anything else?" Chris asked, eying the two children.

"You ever get snowed in up here?" Alex asked the man.

Chris looked up. "A rare occurrence, but it does happen. During Christmas, our lodge had to shut down operations for an entire week; our guests were not at all happy about the conditions, but, we offered them free lodging at a future date of their choosing."

"That's too bad," Corrina commented.

"Yeah," Alex agreed. "But at least you were kind enough to offer free lodging, that's something, considering this place is pretty high in rates."

"Oh yes, we make sure to keep our guests happy and satisfied during their stay. If for some reason this snow we're seeing now worsens, we generally will close up the shops and restaurants—just to warn you ahead of time—send our staff home to avoid any accidents that may arise during the long drive down the mountain."

Alex nodded. "It was a bit of a slog."

"It gets pretty bad on that road," Chris told him. "Plow can't keep up at times. And with the ice, it's very dangerous for traffic." Chris paused a moment. "Will there be anything else I can do for you?"

"Nope," Alex said, scratching his signature to the paper forwarded to him over the counter. "That'll do."

As they turned to leave, Chris shouted, "Enjoy your stay at White Cap Lodge, where the snow is plentiful and the fun is forever! And Happy Birthday Caleb Henning!"

"What a weird guy," Caleb said to his father, not daring a glance behind.

"A bit strange," Alex said.

"He's just a nice man," Corrina countered. "Imagine speaking to a hundred people a day or more. Eventually, you too would become weird, strained by repeating the same words and phrases to each customer. It could drive somebody to go insane."

"I think he is," Megan snickered in her pink gloves.

CHAPTER 6

"Explain to me again, Colonel, because I'm having a difficult time understanding—or should I say, comprehending, what you have just explained to me."

Colonel Ben Heywood explained it twice. A third attempt would only further stress his already ridiculous summation of what occurred aboard the aircraft. How could a man in his position—a man who had spent nearly half his military career designing classified weaponry for the US government—somehow allow such a catastrophe that resulted in his latest project to be carried by the wind out into the sky, only to drop as a coin down a well? The pilot said they were blowing through a patch of turbulent wind. Said it could affect avionics. It was an understatement. Not only did it affect all those gizmo's wired beneath the cockpit, but it had somehow manipulated the control mechanisms leading to the ramp and paratrooper door. What resulted was chaos.

"I say this only because it's considered proper etiquette questioning such an incident of this unfathomable degree: do you realize what is at stake? Do you realize the danger that will now likely result if this animal is loosed into the public if some malfunction were to occur after impact?"

The face on the screen was a hawk. Unbroken were the eyes that remained slit in sockets black and deep. An immaculate silver top of bristles contrasted with the bronze skin of the face which had become hard as slate under the conditions. General Coy Hall was a man not to be left empty of promises, even ones dashed to fate by wind or war. With a secretary expecting word of the shark, and the disaster which resulted in the loss of the shark, Heywood was a wet piece of meat in the General's sight.

"Without adding insult to the situation—which is difficult considering the circumstances, Heywood—please, delight me; please share with me information that will rectify this atrocious piece of news into something that will assist in lowering my blood pressure to a manageable level?"

Colonel Heywood swallowed, well aware of the general's history of lashing out at subordinates who failed to satisfy, not only with words but in actions that remain shadowy and fatal. "Yes, sir... The beacon, sir, I've tracked it to a location only two hours from our current position."

"And what sort of action have you taken to

recover this multi-million dollar project?" Hall asked, reminding Heywood of the value behind the shark's development and the importance of its recovery.

"Uh, my team, sir, they are preparing to board the bird that will bring them to within fifty meters of the last reading."

"Last reading?" General Hall inquired, making a steeple of his fingers below his chin, leaning back in a chair allowing display of his impressive collection of ribbons pinned to his army jacket; crossed infantry rifle insignia flashed off his lapels. "I'm assuming with this information, the node is inactive? Which means you are unable to track the shark's precise whereabouts, which also leaves the possibility that this shark may indeed have burned up its neuro-chip during the crash—is this correct?"

There was a moment of silence that hung in the air before Heywood spoke in a voice clipped of the usual confidence that was a staple in his character. "Yes, sir. The beacon is no longer pinging location readout, sir."

More silence, but on the General's side. It was a brooding blackness. Gears were shifting in the mind, consequences shaping. "I'm going to be blunt and curt, Heywood, so listen closely as if your life depended on it, because ultimately: it does."

Heywood leaned towards the screen, fearful the general might leap from the pixel field, materialize before him, and throttle his throat, or worse.

"You recover that shark. You make it fast. If you are unable to carry out this mission successfully, well... I needn't remind you of the capabilities at my disposal that will be activated if you fail in your endeavor. Are we crystal?"

He could imagine it alright. The men currently under his command—under his orders—were soldiers. Soldiers followed the commands of their superiors. Trent and his men were a special unit, comprised to carry our highly discretionary military operations—field testing experimental weaponry and equipment that officially did not exist. But at heart, they were soldiers—special forces soldiers. Green Berets. Commandos. Trigger pullers. They held no special allegiance to Heywood; they were merely thumbed under his command during the duration of the project to test and observe the shark and its capabilities and no further. And if he failed, he knew the men would be activated as General Hall pointed out. It was a dangerous game, one he'd been playing for many years now.

"Loud and clear, sir."

"I want the men airborne immediately. Do they have everything they require?"

"Yes, sir! We have additional weapons and gear standing by, sir!"

"Excellent. Now tell me, where is our shark?"

"Last ping was in a mountainous location west of here— Washington state to be precise, a short distance by helicopter. Unknown at this time if there are any civilian population centers in the immediate area of the crash site."

General Hall waved his hand to a figure off-screen. "Contact me the second you and your team are on the ground. I want updates, Heywood—consistent and concise information regarding this recovery effort. I can only stall the secretary so long."

"Yes, sir!"

"Oh, and Heywood—one last thing."

The colonel straightened, bottom lip quivering. "Yes, sir?"

"You have 24 hours."

CHAPTER 7

On his sixth run, Alex was a bright purple bullet; a flashing strike of amethyst lightning, bolting past clusters of skiers garbed in bright colors, much like his own outfit—a gift from his wife the day before they left their home on the outskirts of Seattle. Flushed with purple, the outfit had three bands of white running vertically down the chest and arms, the collar, too, a thick pad of white. His goggles were a chromatic stain of yellow, purple, and green, and his gloves were thick and violet in shade. Now, parting the snow, a flaring trail of ice crystals behind him, Alex worked his poles to avoid the slower skiers who were plenty and crowding the more advanced lanes. A novice himself, he preferred a challenge, even if that meant failure.

The slope was populated. Folks all over were streaking down the mountain, vibrant blurs that contrasted bright on the snow. Pines sagged heavily on the perimeter of the slopes, limbs weighed flat with powder. Flakes continued to hammer the hill and skier alike but did nothing to impede their fun.

Up ahead, a good hundred feet or so, two red flags punched into the snow, indicating a rise. In the past, he'd hit a ramp before, but nothing of the size coming up on him quick. Though he preferred to challenge himself, he figured it best to avoid the ramp like he had the last five runs—a broken leg wasn't something he felt like dealing with in the immediate future. Instead, he leaned to the right, sweeping near as the skier to his front continued along the incline, cutting through the air, making a damn near perfect landing that he celebrated with a whooping shout of pride.

Alex slowed his speed, coming to the end of the slope. Knots of skiers were gathered at the bottom, detaching feet from skiis. Some were animated, chatting about the slope, recalling some moment that almost put them on their ass or wished they could have captured in a photo.

Above him the lift was packed with passengers riding back up the hill, likely for another run. But not Alex, this was his last for today. Corrina made him promise. After all, they had Caleb's birthday to celebrate, the sun would be sinking soon, and that coal-shaded sky would soon become black.

Shaking from his skis, Alex waited his turn, knowing his family was waiting for him at the top. Caleb had tried his hand earlier at skiing, but was antsy about those presents, telling his dad, Can't we just go back to the room, I want to open my presents now, not later.

Alex would say, Don't worry, son, we'll be back in the room before you know it—those presents aren't going anywhere.

Of course, being a young man, patience was thin and easily stressed. Caleb wanted nothing more than to be with those presents, his fingers tearing through paper and box alike.

Megan was too afraid of the slope, which Alex assumed would happen. It was her first time, and being as she was shy about most things, and lacking confidence, she wanted to stay up top, play in the snow, make a snowman, throw snowballs, and stuff of that nature. Corrina was happy to stay with her. She wasn't much of a skier herself, not like Alex. Alex never considered himself a pro or even a good skier, but he enjoyed it—enjoyed the time he could spend on the slope. So, waiting on the lift, he became a bit sour, a bit down that he was finished with today. It'll be okay, he told himself. There's always tomorrow and the next day. Plenty of time to ski and enjoy the slopes!

Taking his seat on the next lift, a voice off to his right turned his head.

It was a woman. A beautiful woman. Blond curls fell down her shoulders, bangs suspended by a thick pink band. Blue eyes, cold and sharp as ice. She was wrapped tight in a pink one-piece spotted in colorful three-dimensional triangles that gave plenty of hints of what lay concealed beneath by all that color. She took a seat next to him, and put those brilliant blue gems on his dark pair. "You mind if I ride up with you?" She pointed a finger up the mountain. "My friends beat me to it."

Alex shook his head. "Not at all, please," he said, moving aside so she could squeeze beside him.

She threw herself next to him, her right knee brushing his own. "Thank you."

As the lift did its job, bringing them high over the packs of skiers below, the snow-dusted their legs and shoulders, poked at their face and mixed in their hair.

"Beautiful out here," she said, admiring the range of snow-capped peaks and white woods that seemed to stretch endlessly to a pale blur in the distance.

"Yeah, quite," he said, doing his utmost not to look over at those two big mounds pushing against that pink one-piece, two triangles incidentally framing her nipples.

"Too bad you can't see the lake from here, it really centers the picture of this place. My name is Kathy," she said, offering a hand.

He took her hand, gloved like his, and pumped it once. "Alex."

"Nice to meet you, Alex," she said, then smiled —a somewhat amusing smile. "That's a great outfit you have there."

Alex looked down, almost sheepishly so. "Yeah, my wife's idea. Figured she'd get me something bright—distinguishable—something she could pick me out in I guess."

lift," he admitted.

"Have a nice little chat on the way up?" she asked, a bit of poison in the words.

Alex shifted uneasily. "Nothing personal, if that's what you're getting at."

Caleb ran up with Megan. "Dad, can we please get to the room now!"

Alex smiled. "Yeah, son, let's get to that room," he put a hand out to his wife, thankful for his son's intervention, "Shall we?"

The fire in her eyes dimmed to a smoldering pit. She may have had some other things on her mind to express, but dropped whatever it was, figuring it best to avoid conflict on her son's birthday.

"Yes, let's get to the room, sweetheart."

"I'll only be a minute, just wait over there," Tabitha told her boyfriend Johnny.

"Come on babe, can't you hold it until we get to the room?"

"Unless you want me to piss myself, no—no, I can't hold it until we get to the room."

"Fine," Johnny said.

Tabitha wandered from the slope and made Johnny watch over her gear as she found a good spot in the woods to pop a squat. Nervous some skier would catch a glimpse of her naked bottom, she brushed aside snow-thick limbs, reaching a spot that she felt would be adequately distant from lurking eyes.

A good fifty feet into the woods, the pines were dense, the snow heaped plenty, and a wind blew through there that put her nipples to hard and her skin to leather. Taking a quick peek, not seeing anything but piles of snow and pines with sagging limbs, she worked the baggy yellow trousers down around her shins, slipped her panties down, and lowered herself. A hot line of piss burned the snow below her. The wind brushed through her long dark hair, and a snap of a branch brought her eyes.

"Come on," she urged herself.

Something else caught her eyes the moment she went to stand and fix herself—something just in front of her. It took a moment for her to understand just what in the hell she was seeing as she ran the zipper up on her ski pants. It was a bit funny looking, the snow bulging like that. But it stopped being so funny after that bulge became a streaking column that lashed towards her with a speed that would have caused a scream had it not been for the thing that exploded out of that long bulky column in a misty white cloud. Something with big red eyes like boiling blood and teeth like razored spades. Its jaw unhinged the moment it came out of that pack, swallowed over the top of her, clamped down hard just under her breasts, shearing her ragged from the belly, where it then disappeared into the snow, leaving Tabitha and her legs to twitch and spill reams of blood and entrails in the cold.

"Tabitha?"

Johnny heard something and thought it was a scream, so Johnny goes back into those woods, looking for his girlfriend. And when he got a look at all that blood that splashed the white pine limbs, saw those two legs jerking with some strange vitality, blood juicing from the cavity of her belly, loops and—dear God—so much damn blood everywhere it stained the snow like scarlet ink, Johnny screamed. He screamed like Tabitha never had the chance to scream.

He turned to run, get some help, when something big as two tall men jumped out of the snow, white fins and tail whipping in propulsion. A big wide mouth full of blood and pink teeth clamped onto his neck, and pulled his head from his body. Johnny dropped to his knees, his arms up, hands feeling for a head that was no longer there to feel. His fingers dug around, upsetting tissues and vessels, poking at a knob of vertebrae. Blood pissed out of his neck in a high pressure that slashed the pines and snow red around him. He managed to crawl forward a couple of feet before his body locked up and fell headless into the snow, shuddering and pumping out what was left to pump.

CHAPTER 8

Didn't take long to find the canister. It was Lynch that spotted it. Saw the blue dot winking up at him from a cluster of pines just below the helicopter.

The pilot of the Huey circled the area until he located a spot suitable for a safe deposit of Heywood and his men. After a quick search, their boots sank in the snow, the chopper back in the sky, and the team fought drifts and flakes that burdened their movements, much like they had back in Siberia during extraction. But it wasn't so much the gear, weapons, and ammo that each of the men was encumbered with that hampered motion, call it fear. Fear of that shark divorced of its control, fried of its neuro-circuitry, free to hunt and eat without command, prowling the woods in search of blood, waiting in the snow.

Nobody was saying much, keeping silent on the issue.

Heywood, Beretta pistol on his hip, white camouflage pattern parka keeping him warm, black cotton cap, black army gloves, woodland pattern trousers—outfitted like his team—he was working the transmitter, but becoming frustrated with its lack of response. Not that he expected anything since contact with the canister was lost hours before, right after its plunge into the woods. But with that threat looming over his head—General Hall's orders picking at the front of his mind, 24 hours, Heywood—he kept at it, staring down at that bright blue screen, hoping to catch a bleep, anything to indicate the shark was alive, under control, not rogue and depleting the forest of its furry wildlife. But what had his nerves fired, gave his heart a few pained beats, was the ski lodge the team spotted, packed with visitors—parking lot damn near capacity. The thought of that shark reaching the lodge, if it indeed was rogue, then time was crucial. Heywood could imagine the headlines: Slaughter at Ski Resort!, Massacre on the Ice!, Monster in the Mountains!, Shark Bites Confuse Authorities!, Survivors Scream: Shark!, Snow Shark: Strange Aberration of Nature or Government Project?

As the fantastic imagery played behind his eyes, he kept his hopes high, but his belly was squeezing up on him, telling him something bad was about to happen—or already had.

Moving into a small clearing that split the woods back a short distance, the men on his six moved with disciplined silence.

Conditioned from years of experience hunting

guerrillas in murky wet jungles, arming the legions of Allah high up on the jagged spines of colossal peaks in Western Asia, obliterating Qaddafi-backed terrorist training camps in the scorched and burning sands of North Africa, leading a man hunting machine to terminate rebel units beneath the dark canopy of Honduras, to working in tandem with a blood-hungry shark in the frozen wastelands of Siberia, Trent and his commandos were in their element, a natural transition that comes easy with experience.

"What if it's loose?" Lynch asked, voicing a concern that none wanted to think about it.

"What if it is?" Webber said, turning his head over his broad shoulder, snow streaking past his dark face. "Nothing we could do about it. Keep your eyes on the snow; see something funny, call it out, get that weapon ready."

"I heard the skin was bulletproof," Baxter said, his German MP-5K threaded with a sound suppressor sweeping the woods ahead of him getting closer with each step. "How are those tranquilizers supposed to punch through that thing?"

"Ain't a machine; not like that monster of metal back in the jungle," Webber reminded him. "This thing breathes; has gills like any other shark. The hide is tough, but nothing no bullet or needle can't stop."

Baxter shrugged. "You would think maybe with all that technology put into its brain, that they would somehow strengthen its skin; some sort of synthetic sleeve like a ballistic vest. Can't imagine all they vested in it only to get wasted like a man on the battlefield."

"The shark had added protective elements introduced into its hide," Colonel Heywood remarked over his shoulder. "But unfortunately, it can't stop a bullet, though it can absorb a heavy amount of damage, much like a vehicle or tank, before it is rendered inoperable."

"So, we can kill it?" Lynch asked a bit more optimism in his voice now, his CAR-15 poking pockets of pale shade in the woodline.

Heywood stopped and faced him. "It bleeds, sergeant. And like anything that carries blood in its body, it is susceptible to death." He looked over the men, flakes dusting their black caps, forming ridges across their shoulders, settling on their weapons; his brow knitted together. "Unfortunately, as you men are well aware, we have no way to verify if the shark survived the impact. But if it did, and it's alive—its chip unresponsive—we must not bring harm to the shark. The weapons are merely a defensive measure, but by no means are they to be utilized unless faced with imminent peril. That is why each of you was given a tranquilizer pistol. And I trust that you men will have strength enough to employ that pistol when we locate the shark—again, only if it's hostile. The agent works quick—instant paralysis of the musculature system upon injection."

Lynch stepped forward. "But if the shark is loose, sir, how are we to track its movements? Its location? Seems that transmitter in your hands ain't working so well."

Dark shadows etched the contours of his face. Without a word, Heywood turned, crunching snow, heading for the woods, his head down at the monitor, mumbling things none of the men could hear.

"If that thing comes at me," Webber said quietly to the men around him. "I ain't using no goddamn dart gun." He slapped the frame of the MP-5SD in his big hands, and ran a finger up the integral silencer, clearing it of flakes. "I'm emptying this bad piece into that thing."

Baxter and Lynch laughed nervously.

"Cut the chatter men," Trent told them. He waved his arm forward, CAR-15 menacing the woods. "Move out."

CHAPTER 9

"Well, looks like your shark is alive and well, colonel," remarked Webber, staring down at all the blood that stained the snow across the parking lot; the bits and clots of human bone and skin frozen in the snow like lumps and beads of rubies. "Looks to me like this area was hit with a goddamn bomb."

After they located the canister, saw it cracked down the middle, its cargo disgorged, and nowhere to be found, Heywood had himself a small heart complication. It beat at his breast with a pain that felt like molten metal pouring through his valves. He brought up the satellite phone, punched in some buttons, and reached out to General Hall. Told him what he was looking at, and why he suddenly had an urge to seek dry land.

It appears as if the shark is no longer with the canister, sir, he told Hall. And the transponder is not picking up a signal. I'm assuming the neuro interface has malfunctioned.

The men couldn't make out much of the conversation shared between the commanders, but they heard enough of that radio scratching on the other end to understand that the General wasn't in the best of spirits right then.

Heywood looked on the verge of a stroke. He was tapping and shaking at the phone as if something were wrong. Turns out, there was. Some sort of atmospheric disruption prevented his words from getting through. Which was bad. Because he knew without those updates, that General Hall was liable to become unseated and quick. On top of losing the shark—the transmitter essentially a brick—things were not looking too well for the colonel and his recovery effort.

Back in that field of pine with the empty canister, Heywood ordered the men to beat at the snow, thinking the shark could have been tossed out after impact, perhaps confused, out cold. Told the men it could be lying dead in the woods somewhere. But not a single one of the men believed that for an instant. They beat the snow as ordered, but it wasn't with that tranquilizer pistol in their hands, no, it was with a rifle and submachine gun, finger locked on the trigger, ready for that snow to burst apart with a shark whipping behind it, its jaw unhinged, snapping for meat.

The team worked hard, methodical, probing and prodding likely spots, but nothing turned up just heaps and piles of snow, brush, and more snow. Eventually, they found what could have been tracks—a burrowed hollow cut through a thick drift.

Following the tracks a good hundred meters, they worked their way down a slope congested with pines curtained in flakes.

It was at the bottom of those snow bulky pines where the ground leveled out, that the men spotted the gray brick structure of the restroom, snow thrown up against the walls; saw the septic truck topped with snow, and went white as a skinned skull after seeing all that blood and human waste scattered around as if a hurricane of gore swept through the parking lot. The area looked to be some sort of dismounting point for hikers using a vaguely veiled trail head notched in the woods.

Ringing the pile of gore in the snow, the team had trouble averting their eyes. Death was common in their line of work, but knowing what tore into these bodies—what had once been whole bodies—was something new to the mind. Sure, they'd seen that walking machine in the jungle; saw what it did to those rebels and its brutal massacre of that fishing village, but something that ate men—it was a fresh horror the team was finding trouble accepting.

Webber kicked at a lump of red meat, hair mashed into it. "Looks like the shark just...spit it out. What a damn mess."

That's precisely what it looked close to. Like the shark had its fill, spit out what it couldn't keep down.

Lynch shouldered his rifle, his eyes on the snow,

in the woods, looking for something he didn't much want to find. Snow was piling around them in chunky streaks now, obscuring the woods. The sky was a bold smear above, black and heavy with metal clouds. "That thing can be waiting for us right now," he said. "Could be anywhere in this lot, maybe in them trees over there, looking for an opportunity to strike."

"Settle down," Webber told him. "If that thing were waiting on us here, it would have already shown itself; you think it fears us?"

Lynch shook his head. "Suppose not; but it has intelligence, maybe it knows we're armed, a threat to it."

"It knew those men were armed back in Siberia," Baxter noted. "It didn't hesitate then, don't think it would now."

Heywood had his eyes on the mess. He brought up the transmitter box, started working dials, smashing buttons, hopeful there would be a white dot showing him the shark and its location, but there was nothing there—not like he expected there to be, but he was ever hopeful for a sign. Again, he tried his luck with the satellite phone but quickly gave up after no such luck presented itself.

"How many you think it ate?" Lynch asked, looking at the pile of blood and meat and bone in the snow.

Trent had taken it upon himself to check over the rig, prodding the interior, poking the snow around the tires with his rifle where the build-up was thick.

"Two men," he called out, his eyes inside the rig.

Webber crunched over, followed by Lynch and Baxter.

"I got two cups," Trent pointed at the console where a pair of green paper cups sat amidst a clutter of food wrappers and an ashtray packed with cigarette filters.

"Damn," Webber said examining the truck, catching the name painted on the side. "Emptying a toilet, you never think to fear a damn shark coming out of the woods; maybe a bear, a mountain cat, but not a goddamn shark. Can't imagine what those two must have been thinking."

"I'm sure they were too busy screaming to think much of anything," Baxter told him.

"Wonder where it went?" Lynch asked, his weapon following the timid glare in his eyes looking out across the lot.

"The lodge," Trent said suddenly, thinking back to that broad resort on the hill. "My money is that thing got wind of that lodge. Can't explain it."

The men looked at one another, each with a face as grim as the last.

"Call it intuition," he added.

"Goddamn," Webber shook his head. "It'll be a slaughter."

Boots crunched near the team. It was Heywood, more pale than usual. "That's precisely what we'll have on our hands, men. We must reach that lodge quick. I just hope we're not too late."

A sound just beyond the pines that curled along the parking lot from the forest road drew each man's eyes. It was a familiar sound, so no weapons were shouldered in reaction. A flash of movement caught in the gaps of the woodline made them tense.

"What's the plan?" Webber asked Trent, suddenly critical of this new threat.

"Hold your ground, we ain't the enemy here."

Lynch cocked his head. "Sounds like a truck."

Heywood sighed. "Great, just what we need: interference from a local. Have your men push forward," he told Trent. "I don't want that vehicle in this lot."

"Understood, sir."

Trent ordered Baxter into a knot of pines and brush near the entrance; told him to sit tight, and provide security in case they should need it. The remaining three men stood in a loose crescent near the mouth of the narrow entrance, weapons low, snow packed at their ankles, pines on either side tall and blanketed.

Trent's eyes narrowed as headlights swept over the snow, and flashed his eyes. It was a vehicle—V8 from the sounds of it. It was slowing down, easing into the lot. A white Bronco, blue and red light bar sat on top. The lights came on, splashing the snow with color. It came to a stop, an older man stepped out with a bit of haste behind him, pistol in his black-gloved fist. Shielding his head was a wide-brimmed black stetson, collecting flakes on the rim, a brown coat with a wool collar pulled up around his neck, dark blue jeans, and thick brown boots. A brass badge winked off his chest.

"Put those weapons in the snow!" he ordered, his voice loud and booming.

Trent and his men did no such thing. No words were exchanged, just the silence of three heavily armed men as if they were posted at a checkpoint in some third-world hole, snow coating their gear and weapons.

The man came forward, hammer drawn back. "I said put those goddamn weapons in the snow—now!"

Heywood came forward from behind the team, his palms up, facing the man, giving him a startle. Blue and red flashes painted his movements through a wall of dense flakes. "We're not hostile, sheriff. No reason to get all jumpy—"

"You put those weapons down, or I'll put 'em down for ya!" The threat was in the pistol that kept a rigid bead on the colonel crunching towards him.

"Sheriff, my name is Colonel Ben Heywood, US Army, mind telling me your name for diplomatic sakes?"

The sheriff looked from the men to the colonel and took a moment to speak as if he were judging the situation. "Robbins—Orris Robbins—sheriff around these parts."

"Sheriff Robbins, we have ourselves a dire situation in your jurisdiction. Unfortunately, I'm going to have to ask you to lower that pistol, we're no threat to you—we're all friends here, I can assure you of that."

"Either your men put those weapons in the snow, colonel Heywood, or I'm putting you and them in the snow, permanently."

"No reason for threats, sheriff," Heywood told him, keeping his voice tight and even. "I'll be honest with you. We're tracking a killer, loose in these parts. A bad one, sheriff. We have reason to believe that killer could be heading to the lodge we saw on our way in."

"White Cap?"

Heywood nodded. "If that's the name of the resort we spotted on the hill. We have to hurry, sheriff, those people could be in danger at this very moment."

Robbins looked unconvinced. "While we're waiting on my deputy to reinforce this situation we have here, why don't you explain to me the danger these people are facing?"

"I'm afraid without cooperation, sheriff Robbins, that I am unable to impart the information you require."

"Looks to me, colonel," Robbins shook his pistol free of snow, "That I have the upper hand in this situation, so I'm gonna ask you once more why the army is poking its nose in my woods."

"Very well," Heywood said after a pause. "What we're after is not a man nor is it a woman, but something animal."

CHAPTER 10

One moment she was carrying her baby, all bundled for the snow, headed back to the lodge. The next moment, mommy was a big red-clotted smear that stretched a good forty or fifty feet through the pines.

Peter was on his knees in the snow, his hands pressed to his head, screaming the whole time, helpless. Something big burst from the snow; something with a gaping mouth crammed with rows of big sharp teeth like something a child would draw. It was like some immense bear trap, only it wasn't made of metal and springs, but of flesh—pale flesh tough as leather. It snapped over his wife; those big monster teeth breaking her bones apart, blood blowing out of her from a hundred lacerated gashes. Baby Chelsey went flying from her momma's arms as if she were spring-loaded, landing in the fresh white snow with a piercing cry that went right over her own mother's. Next thing you know, Peter had to watch his wife, Kelly, cut down to cuts of wet meat, pieces of bone spilling out of her with lumps of big red and pink loops coiling and pissing fluids in the snow. After, she was taken through the snow —dragged a ways back. Then, what was left of her head, which wasn't much-considering half of her face had been chewed through, sank beneath the white waves of snow, blood bubbling out thick gummy streams of brain and skull.

Peter went to his baby after the shock had begun to fade.

Father's instinct kicked in.

He went over there, crawling, forgetting how to use his legs.

Baby Chelsey was spastic, her cries were cutting right through his heart. Images of his wife were vivid and repeated behind his eyes. He put his hands on Chelsey and started to scoop her from the cold snow when all that snow pillowing her back exploded in a powdery white vapor. A hot pain shot through his arms, detonating with agony in his mind.

After all that snow settled back to the earth, Peter was looking at a great wide shimmering pool of blood splashed around him. In his pain, he failed to notice that his baby was no longer making that whining, squealing sound no more. Where she had been crying in the snow was now a big red hole steaming with meat and tiny bones.

That's when he felt funny, felt like he had that one time when he cut himself too deep, nearly taking a finger from his hand in a circular saw accident.

His lids drew back on eyes insane when he saw the two stumps where once there were hands. Blood was winging out of those cracked open stumps, painting the snow in long red slashes for a dozen feet. Peter screamed into the black sky—screamed for help, but he was too far from the lodge and he knew it—too far from any of the skiers that were left on the slopes.

Peter raised himself, trying his damn best to make it back to that lodge which was a good couple hundred feet through the pines. He could see all the lights inside; all those windows were bright and yellow, and snow was still coming down with no end in sight. There was a rumble in the sky.

"HELP!" he shouted, but it was a weak shout, shallow of strength and breadth one would expect from a grieving father.

The snow bulged off to his left, Peter yelped much like a dog would after somebody stepped on its tail.

Some would say he would look funny running the way he was: no hands, blood spraying from his wrists, hysterical with madness, the way all that snow sank up to his knees, trying and crying his way forward. But not Peter, no, there was nothing funny about it at all. Suddenly, his boot got stuck. Next thing you know, Peter went face first into the snow. Naturally, he used his hands to push himself from the ground, but all that did was bring out a high wailing scream to rise above the woods, lost in that big black sky. But it was cut short the moment he saw that tall white dorsal cutting through the snow; saw the flaming embers of burning red eyes, then saw the thing rise above the surface, its mouth partially open, snow filing down its throat.

"SSHHAARRKK!"

It leaped full out of the snow. Peter saw it. Saw every detail of it. Saw its tough hide, saw those razor fins, and most of all saw those eyes, charged with neon and hunger. Those teeth, rows, and rows of teeth only a monster in his wildest boyhood fears could possess. The whole thing was a flashing animation that bolted at him like a strike of pale lightning.

"NOOOO—" Peter's shout of terror was an echo in that yawning mouth of bloody spikes. It closed over him, squishing him into a wet, juicy jelly—much like a cluster of red grapes crushed under a steel press.

CHAPTER 11

It was endless, the number of soldiers falling to the spread of burning red balls in their paths, or were they mercenaries—perhaps hive-controlled synthetics designed to repulse the invader? Not only did the soldier have to contend with a seemingly illimitable legion of suicidal madmen armed with automatic rifles; mortars launched from the black jungle, and invidious assassins flinging bomb canisters in his path, but of those machine cannons. The multi-barreled weapon systems emerged from cleverly disguised coverts in the jungle floor, springing without warning, as if the commando had triggered some hidden wire or nodule beneath his boot. Caught in its path, the burning bolts would soon atomize flesh into a cloud of red particles to be carried on the contrails of wind blowing in from the sea below the cliffs if one was not quick to avoid its terrible path.

Already had the commando hacked and butchered his way through a hundred men and machines, perhaps twice that number. Most had absorbed the weapon's projectiles, only to expand

and blow apart as if hit with warheads and not pulser beams designed to burn flesh, and bullets—ever faithful in their lethality.

The broad-chested commando, blue band below his blond hair, reached a great wall of steel and machine, a barrier that prevented his breach into the command center. A big ball of red, like the eye of some cybernetic monster, gleamed with a malefic intent at its center. On either side of that big neon ball, projected silver repeating cannons that poured out a ceaseless stream of molten bombs that burned the jungle with flame. A man soon emerged on the precipice of the looming silver rampart. A rifle in his hands kicked against his shoulder as bullets punched into the jungle around the bulk of the American commando, who carefully avoided each well-aimed shot intended to rid this intruder of his plans to destroy Gomeramos, King of the Black Stars.

Returning fire, the commando's weapon cycled madly. A specialized energy rifle found in an airborne cache; its projectiles were a wall of plasma that burned men down into bubbling muculent piles and sank into the skin of metal with the incision of hot blades cutting wax. One such ball found its target. The man above screamed as the plasma consumed his body, incinerating the man's anatomy down into a slimy, smoking, jelly. Concentrating on the glowing red orb, the commando lowered himself amongst the burning jungle floor, his weapon hot as numerous plasma beads punched gaping liquefying holes in the steel wall, smashing into the crimson eye. A roaring explosion ripped apart the jungle with blossoming bursts of flames and metal following the destruction of that seemingly mad eye, gashing the rampart down the center, allowing the commando to proceed into the pit of that ruined machine.

"YES!" Caleb shouted on his feet. "Finally! Six tries, but I finally killed the first boss!"

Contra. His best friend back at school, Ricky Parson, told him that Contra was the best damn game put out on the Nintendo. Said it was about killing aliens and big monsters, said there was some evil syndicate runnings things, name of Red Falcon. He wasn't positive, but he also told Caleb the final boss was a giant demon heart. The first thing Caleb learned about Contra, was that it was damn hard, but nowhere near the punishment of Ghosts and Goblins. Supposedly there was a code floating around, an extension of life code; thirty lives added to the simple three you were given at the beginning. Caleb sure wished there was some way to call Ricky Parson right then, he was sure to know that code. He knew everything about video games. But, sadly, Ricky was visiting his grandmother, so using that phone over there next to his bed would be out of the question.

After he tore open that box of blue wrapping during the party, and that Nintendo was looking back at him, Caleb became a grinning boy again.

He wasn't much for the snow, that was something his dad and mom were enjoying more than his sister and himself. On closer inspection, he saw that this particular model came with two games inside the box. Super Mario Bros and Duck Hunt. He played both at Ricky's house; had plenty of fun clipping ducks with the light gun and leaping on the flagpole that Ricky told him he had jumped over one night. Caleb wasn't sure it was possible. Already he had tried his hand a dozen or so times on the first level. Each time it looked as if Mario were about to clear that brass knob on top, he would sort of lean back as if he'd run into a wall. But Caleb could care less. Maybe one day he would get it. All he cared about now was Contra. He was happy his parents had decided on getting his sister something, only so she would leave him alone, and so she wouldn't feel left out. Megan got like that. Saw her brother get all those gifts on his birthday, yet she was staring off with glassy eyes, ignored. Sometimes she would throw a tantrum, but it was becoming rare with age. This year they hadn't left her out of the gifts. She had two presents; one, the new Barbie she had been asking for, and two, a Cabbage Patch Kid—a big ugly plush with curls of yarn for hair and shit brown overalls and a yellow flower pattern shirt. It was good enough for her.

Proceeding to the next level, it wasn't long before confusion set in at the design which was in complete contrast to the side-scrolling action he'd been struggling through. Now, it was set up more like one of those racing games; some sort of weird point of view. The next thing he knew, soldiers were jumping and flipping on the screen past a barrier of thin white voltage beams. It was the bombs that got him after he figured out how to go prone. The blinking canisters rolled into him, killing off his last life.

"DAMNIT!"

"Caleb!" Alex shouted from the other side of the wall. "Watch your mouth!"

"He really does love that game," Corrina said, wrapped tightly in a terrycloth robe, red curls down each shoulder, one leg bare and clean as polished ivory. She was concentrating on a stack of Polaroid photos she had snapped during the party. "I love the way he looks right here," she pointed out. Captured in the center, the flash perfectly caught Caleb as his lips spread wide, revealing a mouth full of bright white teeth, green eyes round, pupils on the Nintendo box just below his dimpled chin. His hair, dark and thick, was a mess.

"I knew he would like it. He'd been asking for that Nintendo since he turned twelve," Alex said, working the controls on the hot tub, bringing the water to a perfect heat as jets of propulsion churned the surface into a boiling maelstrom. "I was lucky to get that raise."

"Is it ready?" Corrina asked, setting aside the pictures.

"Nearly."

Corrina watched her husband work the

controls. She had been waiting for this moment. Waiting to be alone with her husband. She had some things on her mind, plenty of dirty little things she wanted very much to be doing with her husband, and to him. She was mad at him the moment his bright outfit crested the crown of the hill, and saw him sitting next to that pretty blond girl who was a good ten years younger than the both of them. Corrina, like her husband, was pushing forty, but Alex always told his wife she hadn't aged but maybe a day since he first laid eyes on her back in high school. It wasn't like anything had taken place between Alex and this snow bunny. But something about seeing him there, grinning, laughing with that girl, drew the wind out of her chest. She wouldn't call herself jealous, maybe just a bit insecure about her body. Not like she had a valid reason she would tell herself. Her husband had found her body smooth and curved all in the right places. He always grabbed a hold of her, playing around; squeezing her, pinching there. She liked it, but never really said much about it. But tonight she would finally have some peace with her husband—as much as she could with the kids being in the next room. But they were busy. Caleb would probably end up playing that Nintendo all night. Which was fine with Corrina, just the distraction they would need to make a little noise in their room. Megan was a different story. She could get a bit clingy, but after receiving those gifts, she hadn't much needed her mother by her side. She was busy playing with her dolls; drawing, reading, all that good stuff.

"Oh, I think it's ready," Alex said.

Corrina smiled as her husband pulled off his shirt, and tossed it on the ground. He wasn't much in the sculpted sense, but he was athletic, slim from all that bike riding. His brown hair was still a bit damp from the shower they shared after getting settled into their room, giving it a black shade that hung around his ears in jet blades. Back muscles popped out on him as he reached an arm down to test the water. He had a pair of blue trunks on with red bands down around the knee. He slipped those free. Corrina smiled, getting a good look at that dimpled set of cheeks. He climbed inside, lowering himself, making noises as the heat sank up to his waist. He turned to look at her.

"Oh, babe, it is so hot in here. Feels good after being outside."

Corrina pinched her robe closed as she crossed the room.

Swinging back the shared door, she peeked inside the children's room. Megan looked up from a scattering of papers and crayons and markers, her new dolls seated next to her on the bed. Caleb was focused on that game, tense and shooting his way through pixelated soldiers up the cliff of some blue waterfall and green cliffs.

"Just checking on you guys," she said. "You okay over there, sweetheart?" she asked Megan.

"Yeah, I'm just playing with my dolls and

drawing."

Corrina smiled. "How about you, birthday boy?"

"Fine mom, love the game." It was like one word strung together is how it came out.

"Dad and I are about to watch a movie, so...we'll be busy. Knock if you two need anything."

Megan smiled, then went back to her coloring, her twin red tails of hair falling alongside her cheeks.

Caleb just grunted after his character took a bullet.

Corrina sealed the door and secured the bolt.

"They're just fine," Corrina whispered, more to herself, knowing her husband wouldn't mind as much.

Alex had dimmed the lighting in the room; threw the drapes back on the big picture window set above the hot tub. It had a great angle of the mountain, but with all that black sky and powder, it was hard to see much of anything. Down on the slopes, the lights were blinking off the lift in-between all that heavy snowfall washing past.

"Would have been a much better view if we could at least see the moon," Alex commented, leaning back in the tub, water bubbling around his chest.

"I imagine it would look beautiful with the moon," Corrina agreed, strolling forward.

"Babe, you need to get in here—"

Alex had his jaw dragging on the rim of the tub the moment he turned back, and got a look at his wife. He had seen her a thousand times, but with that soft amber light painting her body, it was like she had just emerged from the canvas of a masterpiece. It was those breasts he was drawn to. Soft, the nipples spongy from the cool air in the room, a perfect handful. A small patch of red hair between her legs. She smiled at him with those eyes—sharp emerald chips that looked on him with a salacious craving.

She put her foot on the stool leading into the tub, her other leg coming up, her toes sinking past the hot bubbles. "Oh, wow—really warm."

"Yeah," was all Alex said, but it came out in a whisper.

Both legs straddling her husband now, she lowered herself down onto him, working the meat of his shaft with her fingers. She gave him another one of those smiles before guiding that pulsing wand between her thighs.

His eyes rolled over white at the feel of his wife. He knew it would be fast, it always was. She knew what he liked, and she gave it to him. It was the moans she was so good at. Sultry, hot, and throaty. The water slapped at her breasts as she worked her hips, and splashed over the rim. Alex cupped her breasts, pulled his wife to him, took a nipple in his mouth, and nibbled at it until she moaned a bit louder.

As the water agitated with their sex, outside that window, above the mountains in the black sky, the lashing of a blue bolt licked the earth, followed by a rumbling groan that shook the foundation of the lodge.

CHAPTER 12

Sheriff Orris Robbins couldn't quite wrap his sixty-odd years around what sort of lunacy this colonel Ben Heywood was laying out for him. It was something a patient of some medical disorder in the skull would lecture him about. Tell him there was some sea monster in the mountains hunting men, on a path of death.

Shark. A goddamn honest to God sea creature tearing through the snow in the goddamn mountains. Sounds a bit funny. Like something a child would come up with. Maybe a group of boys scaring another of their age, telling him to be careful building a snowman out near those woods, because a man-eating shark haunts the snow; likes to lurk among the trees, seal its teeth around little boys, drag them into those deep black woods.

It was a joke. Well, it should have been anyhow. But those glassy black beads the colonel was staring at him with were dead and flat. There was no sort of humor in those eyes. He told Orris many things. Made him swear to oaths on the punishment of blood. Told him if he were to ever reveal these esoteric glimpses into a world he had never known, that he might as well swallow his gun because he would have men coming for him. Said those men would do awful things to him and whichever family he still had kicking on the old proverbial tree.

Peeking at those men packed in the back of his truck as his wheels spun and fought the snow up that mountain, he understood the colonel meant business. It would be a fatal error to doubt the man.

But a shark? In the goddamn snow? In the goddamn woods? Comic book fantasies and trashy horror cassettes are all it was! How could a shark survive outside the sea? Outside the salty depths? Made no sense. Heywood told him it didn't have to make sense, and even if he were to explain to his feeble old fool mind the intricacies involved in the science of its creation, he was sure to scratch at his head like some jungle ape trying to make sense of a dildo. At least, that's how sheriff Orris Robbins took the insult.

The first thing sheriff Robbins did once seated behind the wheel, was pluck that radio from the dashboard, and thumbed the mic—but Heywood cut him off. Told him a few things before he started losing his tongue about some murderous shark in the snow. Made him promise he would somehow thwart his deputy, tell him to return to the station —that all was well and there was no need for his assistance.

Orris fed his deputy some bullshit, but it was enough to convince the young trooper to swing his truck back down the mountain. But how long that would last, say if Orris weren't reporting his status to dispatch regularly, he couldn't say. It was quite probable his deputy would take it upon himself to investigate, something that was nagging at the back of his mind, fearing for the young man's life, uninformed of the danger that lay ahead.

Orris put a few questions to the colonel after they had allowed a group of vehicles to pass them on the snow-packed road—likely staff from the lodge returning home. It was common practice for the resort once the snow had no real end in sight. It was a good thing he had barricaded the trail lot, swinging the gate closed and clamping a lock on its hasp, less some weak bladder needing to relieve itself and happen upon a sea of gore. Orris asked the colonel what was to happen if some late-night arrivals should head up the mountain, to the lodge. Heywood just looked at him with a look that wasn't quite sane and told him they would deal with that when the time came. Orris had no clue what exactly he meant by that, but he didn't like it. Didn't like this man one bit. But, considering there wasn't much a man in his position could do about it right then, he simply carried on.

The truck ground the snow into fine powder as they surmounted the summit. It was black outside, invaded by a wall of white beads thick as marbles. Something shook at the ground.

"Storm coming in," Robbins said, easing his rig around a depression in the road. Bold shades flushed the breach between columns of snow-stressed pines looming in tight clusters on either side of the narrow road. Snowflakes clogged the blades of his headlights.

Frustrated at the lack of connection available with the satellite phone, Heywood looked out the windshield, up into that boiling black cauldron of a sky. "How long is this storm supposed to last?"

Robbins shrugged. "Beats me—wasn't supposed to be no storm like this moving in. Supposed to be mild snowfall, nothing more."

Flickering blue lights crawled behind the black screen in the sky. Thunder shook the mountain.

"Just what we need," Heywood sighed, "more issues."

The colonel was not only in a tight spot with the recovery effort but his impatience at his inability to communicate with General Coy Hall was getting the better part of his sanity. He was also well aware of how thin Hall's patience could be when dealing with men, fathoms below his rank, who were unable to properly carry out simple orders. Besides that ruthless white hunter in the snow, Heywood had to worry about those men seated in the rear, just behind him. Would they suddenly come alive, activated as if they were, put a hole in his face? Maybe they would wait until he was outside, in the woods, nothing but ice and black and cold gusts of wind howling and shrieking, beating at his face with flakes, blinded. That would be a good time. When he was most miserable, not in this truck with the heat going—comfortable. Heywood was becoming paranoid and figured he had good reason to be.

Trent and his team sat in silence. Men checked over their weapons, clearing ice and drops of water collecting in chambers; correcting any deficiencies that could land them in serious trouble once it came time to put those weapons to work. Bolts locking back on plugged chambers was not something you very much wanted to be dealing with when your life was hanging out there, bullets snapping and whistling close to your scalp. But out there, in that snow-blown black world, there would be no enemy shooting back at them. No traditional enemy anyhow. There was something worse out in those white wastes. Something predatory, mean, hungry—pernicious. Heywood designed that thing to eat. Designed it to smell blood, find that blood and crush meat with those special teeth he was so adamant about replacing with its naturally grown set.

"Here we are," Robbins said. Headlights plunged into the parking lot. Rows of vehicles sat like boulders bulked with snow thick on the hood and top, tires buried past the rim.

"Where do we go from here, Colonel?" Robbins asked, easing his rig into the lot.

Heywood looked out across the lot, looked up at that great brown structure like something put together on a canvas with oils and paints, the perfect winter lodge. A hundred windows looked back at him. Some were glowing, most of which were black as the night. Lightning whipped at the overlapping mountain peaks in blue stripes.

"Now we look for our shark."

CHAPTER 13

It had been a long day, but nothing he wasn't much used to at that point. Been working White Cap since he was twenty years old. Six years later, he was a supervisor, working the front counter, long hours—so nothing much had changed, except the pay increase. Thing was, at times like this, when the snow was plenty and the hill all but unnavigable, it was a bit of a kick in the old bag. In all honesty, Chris hated this job. But only took it because he loved the outdoors; loved to ski. An added benefit to the job was he got to hit the slopes free of charge. But it was the people that he most found unpleasant, who put a dent in his mood. There were some real characters that filtered through the day. Most got on his nerves, acting as they did. Others were in good spirits, honest and caring folks who respected his position and never once showed disdain for his employment choice and the limits of what he can and cannot offer them.

A flame bloomed in his fist, sucked into the

hand rolled plugged between his lips. He pulled deep and blew out a jet of acrid-fumed smoke.

"Finally," he said.

It was good stuff. A perfect yield he had grown from a seed plucked from a bag of green he'd bought a few months back. The stress was getting to him. He had orders to shut down the lodge services a couple of hours back, told to send crews packing and get down that mountain before the snow swallowed them up. Left with only a handful of staff, their jobs would become that much more difficult once daylight recessed some of this encroaching dark.

He took another long drag and blew it out.

He started thinking about them kids from earlier, the birthday boy. Wished he could go back in time, back to those days when not a lot mattered. Only video games and toys and fun, not bills and all that assorted bullshit that seemed to pile higher and higher with age. He hated to put on that mask—that facade—when people came around, but he did it because that's how he got up there in position and pay. Hated saying those little things—things like Happy Birthday, have a nice day, enjoy your time, best slopes in the state, and that terrible jingle that followed each signature of a guest.

Another long pull of the smoke filled his lungs.

Headlights spilled through the lot. The sound of a heavy motor purring through the snow. Flakes stroked the night, so making out that roving bulk of a vehicle was near impossible. He knew it was highly unlikely to be a visitor at this late hour—what with this storm swallowing up the land. Also considering he had phoned Reggy down the hill, a buddy of his who worked nights at a small inn at the foot of this big mountain, told him to put out the sign—a sign that informed late-night guests that the lodge was packed and full, and there was no need to waste thirty miles of gas on a chance; unless for some reason he had forgotten to put it out, but he doubted that. Besides, this sound had a familiarity to it. Heard it hundreds of times.

He took another drag and held it in.

"Shit," he said to himself after catching a glimpse of the bronze star painted on the side. "Sheriff Robbins."

The truck was moving slowly as if it were patrolling, moving with a cautious grace. Two bright bulbs painted the entrance, causing Chris to shut an eye, and put a hand in front of his face.

A door swung open. Robbins, still inside the cab, yelled out over the hood. "Get back inside, Chris!"

Chris pinched the weed and shoved it in his pocket. With a hand blocking the headlights, he said, "Sheriff Robbins? I can't understand you."

Walking into the lot, shielding his brow from the snow, he hurried over to where the rig sat idling, windshield wipers carving flakes.

"Get back inside! Get out of the snow!" Sheriff Robbins told him again, in a heavy-handed voice he hoped the young man could understand.

"Back inside? The snow?" Chris asked, quizzical at the order.

Robbins ducked back inside the truck and grabbed his flashlight.

"Don't even think about it," Heywood told the sheriff. "That thing can be out there right now."

Robbins scoped the lot and wasn't seeing anything but a bunch of snow. But it wasn't all that deep, so the possibility of not seeing something in it was minimal at best.

"If I see it, I'll run back, that snow there is shallow—look," he pointed to Chris. The snow was just below his ankles.

"Make it quick," Heywood told him. He looked to his men. "Get those pistols ready. If you see it, do not hesitate."

Trent and his men would have no problem forgoing hesitation. They weren't a bunch of raw recruits, fresh from the sandy pines of Ft. Benning. They were tested men. Had their boots in more soils on this earth than most would ever learn about. These men were a collection of history. To think they would hesitate in the face of that thing was a grave underestimation. Were they scared? You bet they were. Trent had himself a touch of silver in that dark hair since Siberia. But would that prevent their reaction from reaching out and punching that demon full of holes? No—it would only invite a maelstrom of flinging brass and burning lead.

Colonel Heywood brought out his silver dart

gun, drew the safety off, and cracked open the door a wedge. Snow was pulled inside, and a cold wind put bumps on his skin and put a shiver in his bones.

Chris looked on the sheriff. "Something wrong, sheriff? You look a bit spooked."

Yeah, Orris Robbins looked spooked alright. Something about that twitch in his eyes; the way that beam of light in his hands kept flickering because his nerves were on edge.

"You need to get back inside, Chris," he told him, swinging that yellow beam around the lot. "Something bad is going on up here." He nodded his head back to the truck. "Got some people in there, important people. Say they're hunting something up here that has hurt a lot of folks."

Chris could have laughed. Maybe it was the weed, but there was something funny about Robbins. Like the way he spoke; that twitch pulling at his eye. Maybe it was the way he kept stabbing that light around the lot, leaning over, crouching, sweeping the undercarriage of car, truck, and van. It was a bit…strange to see the man detached from his usual, hard-ass self.

"I don't understand," Chris said, keeping a good distance from the law in case that weed had decided to put its odor out there.

"Ray," Robbins shook his head, thinking about all that blood mixed in the snow. "He's dead. Benny, too."

"Ray? Septic Ray?" Chris asked. "What the hell

happened?"

"Get that boy inside," Heywood shouted from the truck.

Chris looked past the sheriff and tried to get a look at the man seated inside. "Who is that?"

"Chris, you listen to me, you get back inside, lock these doors. Gather whatever staff you have, keep your head about you, and lock this place down."

"I don't understand," Chris shook his head. "Why? What's hurting people?"

Robbins had a look of pain in his eyes. "You wouldn't believe me, son. Hell, I don't know if I believe it myself. Now go on; go inside, hurry up."

Chris turned to leave, not bothering with any more questions.

Movement amongst the vehicles grabbed his attention. Something was moving in the snow, out there in the lot. "Robbins, what's that—"

Robbins swung around, his eyes on whatever had Chris and those eyes of his focused. Snow was pushed aside; bulging and shifting. Orris grabbed at his piece, put his light on the snow, and thumbed the hammer back. "Chris, get inside—NOW!"

It was so sudden. The way that thing launched itself out of the snow-packed between the vehicles. First, there was nothing but black hanging over the lot, cut with streaks of fluffy white flakes. Next thing you know, two superheated glowing red points above a set of pearl white fangs, edged and honed to something worthy of penetrating armor.

Chris screamed somewhere in that split instant the moment those big pointed blades clamped around his body like a giant pale fist. Blood was plenty, and it blew out of Chris like a child squeezing a juice packet empty. Only there was more than just one tiny pinpoint. Had to be six, maybe ten gashes, cut by those hideous flesh pokers. Blood winged and hit Robbins in the eyes. His weapon jumped in his hand, a bullet whistled into the night.

Trent and his team dismounted the truck. Weapons were shouldered.

Lynch watched that young man in his bright green parka crushed into something no longer resembling humanity; something more like you would see on some sun-beaten road, pasted to a fine sauce by a hundred tires. The shark took its time, rendering the man down into clumps and pools. It was choking on the meat, and the sound... too hideous for ears.

"Open fire—" Trent ordered.

"No—wait!" Heywood shouted, that pathetic little silver piece waving in his hands, afraid of losing his shark to a bunch of men who had no compunction with chopping that fish into tiny pieces.

But the order was carried out.

Bullets chewed apart the snow. Men were glowing as flames jumped from the muzzle. Brass piled at their boots as the team emptied their weapons at the monster.

"It ain't fuckin' stopping!" Webber said as he dropped the bolt on a fresh magazine.

Lynch banged out a wild burst that stitched the shark with three holes below the gill. Blood pumped out of the holes, but whatever effect a bullet would have on a man was impervious to this maneater. It continued to chomp, grind, and obliterate that young clerk into a fine and unrecognizable stain.

"CEASE FIRE! CEASE FIRE!" Heywood shouted, going ballistic, nearly throwing himself in front of that copper wall of heat. He was watching on with fear. Not at the fear that would assail any other person looking at that thing feeding, but fear of losing his project; all those years sank into something only to be broken apart right there in front of his eyes.

The shark swallowed its last chunk of bone and meat, wiggling its way deeper into a bank of snow pushed up by the plow earlier in the day.

"It's getting away!" Lynch shouted. His weapon coughed out ten rounds that impacted the snow at its tail, sparking off the concrete below.

"DON'T KILL IT!" Heywood screamed. "YOU WERE ORDERED TO SUBDUE THE SHARK, NOT BRING—"

Trent had enough of this colonel. Defending that thing as it butchered that man boiled his blood. Lowering his weapon, he bolted forward as if released by a catapult. His fingers put a groove in

Heywood's throat. There was fire behind his eyes. Trent was a quiet man. Never one to speak his thoughts too loud. He was a man who acted. And right then, Heywood was quickly figuring that one out.

"You order us not to fire on such a thing," Trent told him, incredulous with the command, his dark eyes sharp. "I have to ask myself what kind of person you must be. To allow that thing to eat a young man who had no reason to die, and you want that thing put to sleep—to study? Sorry, colonel, but my men and I aren't on that level. We see this again, it's good as dead."

"You can't kill it," Heywood said between clenched teeth. "This project is worth more than all of you combined. It will change the face of warfare as we know it!"

"You sound mad, Colonel. But I can't allow that thing to live; it's gone rabid and needs to be put down. This is no area for your little pet to be running trials."

Heywood grinned, spittle on his lips. "It can withstand serious damage—it's too quick for you and your weapons."

"Not quick enough," Lynch countered. "I hit that thing good."

Heywood laughed. "It will take more than a few bullets to put an end to it, young man."

Webber stepped forward, throwing a shadow over the colonel's eyes, tapping at his chest crammed with magazines. "No problem, sir, we have more than a few."

Heywood looked away from the towering bulk of the soldier.

"Mark my words, we'll kill that thing. Your monster doesn't deserve life." Trent released his hand and fumbled with his rifle.

Heywood rubbed at his neck. "You have made a terrible error, sergeant. You—"

"You forget," Trent said, cutting him off. "We may be under your command, but we ain't one of your godless machines. Morals are in our blood. You should have hired mercenaries if you wanted cutthroats."

"You agreed to this project, Trent. You and your team have an obligation to see that this shark is in no way further harmed. We must collect it—that is a direct order from General Hall!"

"You speak as if that thing is waiting on a leash to go for a walk," Trent told him. "That thing is now primal. There is no working chip in that brain; it's doing what its kind has always done. Hunt and eat."

"Precisely why you cannot hurt the subject further. We must recover it—need I remind you of your station, sergeant? You are a soldier. I'm your commander. When I give an order, you follow—whether you agree with that order or not."

"I agreed to observe its actions in Siberia—against our enemies. Not to watch it eat American citizens. You must be out of your goddamn mind, sir. This is no longer a mission of observation. It's termination."

The men rallied behind their leader, weapons hot, faces curled in anger, yet fearful of that snow and what waited in it.

Heywood grinned. "This is insubordination, punishable by chapters you can't even fathom!"

Trent let the bolt fall on a fresh magazine. "Looks to me sir, whatever little threats you have on your mind, ain't gonna cut it out here. This ain't your little lab back in Maryland, sir. This is the battlefield. My word counts—not yours."

Sheriff Robbins stumbled forward, wiping blood out of his eyes. His face and blouse were beaded red. His eyes were a perfect example of horror. "It…it just came out of the snow. Oh Lord, it ate that man—Chris—ate young Chris. I've known him since he started working up here." He put his eyes on the colonel, fingers tightening on the butt of his magnum. "Your goddamn pet did this, colonel. What the hell—"

Movement drew rifle and submachine gun barrels.

Eyes were wide, anticipating.

"It's still there," Baxter said, his weapon on that pile of snow where it sought cover.

"To the building," Trent said.

The men needed no more urging. As a team, they moved. In the middle, Heywood, pushed forward like a prisoner roughed by a contingent of guards, still losing his shit about the treasonous ways of his men. Sheriff Robbins had that gun in his hand, scanning the lot. And before they reached those double doors leading into the lodge, he saw it, much like Benny had seen it back in the truck; saw those two hungry red eyes leering at him from the snow.

CHAPTER 14

Alex could have sworn he heard something he only typically hears from all those action movies playing round-the-clock on Channel 37.

Gunshots.

Yep, that's what it had to be, he thought. But out here? In the middle of the night? Isolated at the top of some mountain, outside of a snow resort? Was hard to make much sense about.

Corrina turned her head, awake at the feel of her husband leaning up in bed. "You okay?"

Alex was up, a white sheet down at his waist. Bare-chested, hair jutting wild. He clicked on a small lamp sitting beside him on the nightstand. "Heard something funny."

"What—what did you hear?" she asked, rubbing at her eyes.

"I don't know, sounded…well, it sounded like gunshots."

Corrina sat up a bit more, tugging the covers up over her breasts. "Are you sure? That's a strange thing. Maybe it was a dream?"

Alex thought about that. Was no dream like that; it was a good dream, full of naked—"Yeah, it is strange, but I'm sure that's what I heard, and it was no dream."

He swung his legs out from beneath the covers. Found his shorts, put his legs inside, and snapped the band at his waist. He padded over to the window. Throwing the blinds back, he looked outside, at the black, at the snow; the ridge was a stain of ink no amount of squinting or light would see at this late hour.

Pulling a shirt down over his head, he thumbed the light on his digital Casio wristwatch. "Just after eleven." He walked over to his luggage and threw the flap back. "I'm gonna check on something." Outfitted in a pair of blue jeans now, he pulled on a lightweight coat, ran the zipper to his chest, and slipped on a pair of sneakers. "Just gonna' ask the front desk what that could have been. Shouldn't be but a minute."

"Maybe you should call instead?" Corrina offered.

Alex nodded. "Good thinking."

Alex plucked the phone and punched in the number. A few rings later he put it back down in its cradle. "Nothing."

"That's odd," Corrina said. "I'm going to check on the kids."

"You do that, I'll head downstairs, see what that noise could have been."

On his exit of the room, he shook the brass

handle of the door, confirming it was locked. If those were gunshots, that could mean any number of things. And making sure his family was secure and safe, was his number one priority.

Out in the corridor, dim lighting bloomed from wall sconces set between each room in the paneling. Framed portraits hung from the walls. Plush beneath his shoes, the carpet was a dark green bar. Down a way, on his right, the beverage and snack machines put their glow on the wall, humming with neon—the only noise in that dim hall.

A man edged around the corner, startling Alex.

Wasn't so much the man, as it was the hardware in his hands. A black rifle crossed over a chest packed with ammo. Woodland pattern combat trousers hugged his legs, black boots squeaked leather below; a bulky white snow coat and black cap completed the outfit.

He let the rifle fall on its sling; his palms up indicating his peace. "Don't be alarmed," the man told Alex. His voice was young, much younger than Alex, under thirty from the sound of it. "You alone?"

Alex nodded, but couldn't find the words in his throat to tell him he had a family back in the room, waiting on him.

"I'm going to need you to calmly come with me, sir," the man said, and it wasn't so much an order as it was like a friend telling you to listen to him and all would be well.

In the split second that man rounded the corner, Alex had been struck by some surreal quality to the situation—much like being aware in a dream and yet having no control of whichever decision you made. Alex found himself moving forward, then caught himself. Stopped.

"My family," he said, heart working its beats up his neck. "Please don't hurt me, I have children—a wife."

"I'm not here to hurt you, sir. I'm afraid I can't tell you much more, only that you and everybody in this lodge could be in danger."

"Danger?" Alex asked, thinking about those gunshots that had brought him out into the hall to begin with—to face a stranger packed with ammo, holding a mean-looking rifle.

"As I said, sir, just come with me, we're gathering every guest into the foyer to explain things."

We're? Alex thought to himself.

Sounds of shouting below the floor worked up and along the walls down the corridor around him. The sounds were not one or two people, but maybe a dozen or more, rising and panicky.

"What was that?" Alex stammered, black dots jumping in his eyes, fearful of the gunman moving toward him—approaching Alex as if he were the danger and that man was looking to contain him.

"Sir," the young man with the rifle said. "Come with me now, please."

If Alex wasn't mistaken, he had seen that rifle

come up a notch.

"But my family…"

"I assure you, sir, all will be well. You have nothing to fear from us. We're here to ensure you and your family remain safe. But I can't do that unless you come with me."

"Who are you?" Alex asked, wondering if maybe this could be a hostage situation, seeing as the man was armed, packed with all that gear. There was enough of it in the news as of late for Alex to believe that maybe this is exactly what that was. Maybe one of those American patriot groups they kept warning the public about. This man in the hall was either part of some terrorist faction or a soldier—but what would a soldier be doing ordering American men and women and children down into the foyer? None of it made any sense. The man's hesitation at divulging his reason for being there, or requiring he come along with him, was putting up a series of red flags in the old noggin'.

"All will be explained soon, sir, just please cooperate."

As if in response to the screams below, doors on either side started wedging open. Curious faces poked into the hall, followed by a piercing scream that tunneled down the corridor—a scream that sparked the fuse to a chaos that even men with guns could not hope to contain.

CHAPTER 15

Not only were the people crawling over each other trying to free themselves of this madman down the hall with a rifle and enough ammo on his chest to put every guest down in a sticky puddle, but the screams that rolled out of their throats came to together in a collective storm of nameless terror. The people had no reason to fear the man, yet seeing him standing there, with that rifle, was all the spark they required.

The moment those people began screaming and shouting, filling the corridor with disorder, Alex hurried back to his room, pushing aside the crowd, pounding on the door, and shouting for Corrina to let him inside.

Lynch was at a loss as to how to react to this stampede coming at him like a freight train of flesh. It amazed him that these people had decided that the best way to get away from the man was to run towards him, screaming and hysterical with sobbing. Got him to thinking, that if he were the enemy, it would be a great and fruitful slaughter.

Looking back on it, it was a terrible idea to

begin with, but what could they do? They had to let folks know that something bad was going on. It was suggested that they gather up what remaining staff there was still on the clock, assist in going door to door, and ease the resulting tension that would follow from seeing armed men alerting people to danger, but limited by their numbers, the staff that remained had all but become far removed from behind their eyes. They saw what happened to Chris outside, saw that thing in the snow chopping him down into a sloppy, beefy porridge that dripped from its snapping bloody jaw in long wet ribbons. So enlisting their assistance was all but out of the question.

Lynch was backed against a wall. He thought about stitching the ceiling with his rifle, but would that help the situation? Or make it worse? The way those people were falling and shoving and screaming, a gunshot in the plaster above would only exacerbate their terror. Turns out though, that some had found an alternate route of escape.

A window shattered at the far end of the hall. The corridor was suddenly hit with a gush of cold that reached inside the building, frosting the crowd with blowing flakes. Coming to their senses, most of the throng that had decided it would be a good idea to trample their way toward the gunman, had taken a sudden detour, and started back into their rooms, or at least rooms that were wide open and available for shelter.

It was a wild scene. Men were rushing ahead,

wives and girlfriends trailing behind; children being dragged by the wrist or carried. Screams were plenty and behind each wracking wail were tear-streaked faces and quivering limbs.

Lynch was struck with an inability to properly decide on what action would best suit the situation.

It was too clear they had made up their minds, decided the man at the end of the hall was a dangerous threat, and that mindlessly running towards that threat would not be in their best interest if they preferred to live. It was like watching a mass of roaches hit with a spotlight.

Lynch saw a group of people clustered about the shattered window down the hall.

"Wait!" he shouted, but knew it was no good. If they hadn't listened before, his voice was sure to only provoke more chaos.

As the corridor thinned out—people ducking back inside rooms, doors slamming with bolts drawn secure—Lynch saw those people by the window begin their retreat outside, lowering themselves out into the cold night.

Lynch flashed down the corridor, rifle held tight into his chest, boots thumping. "WAIT!"

But it was too late.

Most of the group had already made their escape, all but one last person, one leg poised out the window. A young man, late teens, clothed in a pair of red shorts and a white shirt, barefoot.

"Careful now, that's a serious fall," Lynch told

him. "I'm not going to harm you, I only—"

But the boy jumped. Screams blew over the cold carrying into the building.

Lynch dashed forward, put a glove on the window frame, and leaned a look below.

A pile of bodies moaned directly beneath his eyes. Looked like many of them had broken legs or snapped ankles. There were spots of blood in the snow. Most grunted in some agony, some weren't moving at all.

Just then, he saw it: something moving towards the injured in the snow.

Lynch wasn't the only one finding trouble in inspiring the guests to cooperate. Webber, an imposing man in any situation, stood out as a massive bulk of inhuman strength, the MP5SD 9mm submachine in his massive hands more on the side of a children's plastic toy gun than an actual piece of terminal hardware designed to pop skulls. Besides his brutal-looking aspect looming above the crowd, it was that weapon and those curved magazines bunched in his chest rig that brought about all that screaming and shoving and hysteria that compelled those crazed guests to move about in a reckless manner.

He told them it would be okay, much like Lynch had, but, like Lynch, he was finding people weren't really all too happy seeing a giant man with a silenced weapon in his hands, telling them to move in unison in a quiet and timely fashion. Seeing that gun was enough for them to understand that whatever this man's intention was, it couldn't be good.

Things worked out initially as several guests followed those orders, perhaps shocked by the man's immense size and lethal tube in his hands, but were quickly shaken after Webber was pushed aside by a group of men in revolt, staggering him a bit before the crowd went ape shit and started down the steps, the chorus of their boots and feet and shoes pounding the ground like the thunder disturbing the far hills outside.

His attempts at putting a stop to the madness pouring down the hall weren't much better than a substitute teacher trying to calm a class of unruly and wild kindergartners. Instead, he sort of stood there, hoping Trent and Robbins would provide a barrier to their onslaught.

Baxter found that a man armed with a submachine gun, directing others to form a line and march down that hall might have not been the best method. Like his teammates in the other wings of the lodge, his attempts at bringing calm over the situation were no better than their own.

People were dashing down the stairs, screams, and cries of terror whistling out of their throats, hands dragging over the walls, steadying themselves from falling into the mass of threshing and manic limbs. A young girl was curled up in the hall, a victim of stampeding guests, on her knees, crying. Baxter went over there to lend a hand but felt a blow to the back of his head that caused him to swoon drunkenly, bubbles in his eyes. He went down to one knee, shook his head, and saw the girl being dragged away by a big man with a scowl on his face.

"Come on Patricia! Man's a terrorist!" he shouted down the hall, pulling her towards the exit.

Baxter found himself in an empty corridor, screams echoing further downstairs. A terrorist? He thought.

He raised himself, shook his head clear, and started for the exit.

Heywood was unraveling, and quick. Not only was his patience with the troops diminishing, but his mental stress was starting to get the better of him. No longer were his thoughts collected and ordered, that of a competent leader, but jumbled and disoriented. Since Trent put a trail of bruises on his neck, something inside had snapped, some invading sense of lunacy. Seeing these men suddenly turning their backs on the mission was bringing about a change within himself. How could they blatantly reject his orders? It was treason. That's right, treason! That's how Colonel Ben Heywood was seeing their motives. The team was actively preparing to destroy the shark—his project; a project that would elevate not only his status in the world of science, but place a star on his shoulder. Perhaps two! He was promised a command—a command overseeing the development of a new line of man-hunter. He could not allow these men, however crafty and lethal they may be, to intrude and intercept his project in such a fashion. No, he had to think of something, but what possible action could he take that would not find him bound to a chair, lashed with rope, a spectator to his shark's demise?

"What's that racket?" Orris Robbins asked, a weathered and wrinkled hand resting on his gun belt, another thumbing the brim high on his head so he could hear that much better. "Sounds like thunder."

Trent heard it, but knew that ever-growing rumble was not made by elemental war in the sky, its origin rested within the resort and grew more intense with volume by the second. "Not thunder," he said. "Shit."

It was a massive wave of hysteria and fanaticism. A forest of contesting screams and swinging arms and pumping legs. Guests—a gushing column of guests wild-eyed and screaming and shouting and shoving and rampaging their way forward, united in their madness.

There must have been a hundred, perhaps twice

that number, or just a fraction below. A monstrous body determined to crash into the cold winter night; to leave behind the building crawling with armed men, one baffled sheriff, and a staff cowed and gathered behind the front counter as hostages, held as prisoners.

Robbins stepped forward, a single solitary obstacle to their delirium. "WAIT A MINUTE FOLKS, WAIT A MINUTE!"

And he tried, oh good Lord in the high vaulted paradise did he try to get that voice to rise above those marching feet and vociferous roars and screams, but even he was unable to hear the sound, the command, of his straining chords. Twenty-five long years working in these parts, up and down this mountain, and not in one of those long remembered times had he ever seen such disorder in humanity. Robbins was a man who settled disputes, mostly involving property rights and the like; had himself involved in a murder investigation at one time involving a local back down the hill, back in the small mountain suburb of Owin. But never—not once—in one of those years had he to deal with such an issue of this magnitude.

Trent stepped forward, put his rifle on the crowd.

Instantly, the momentum driving their manic flight to escape had come to a sudden conclusion. Some braved the man with the big black rifle, massing forward, but Trent swung that cold black muzzle into those frightened, yet, daring faces—urged them back with a look in his eye.

"Listen," Trent addressed the stunned faces. "We are not here to inflict harm on any one of you. Nor are we a hostile force. We are soldiers—American soldiers." He put his eyes on Heywood a moment and saw something in that gleaming glare brooding in those drawn sockets. Looking back at the crowd. "There's something bad on this mountain. Something hurting people." Seeing no reason to sprinkle sugar on shit, he continued. "People have been killed. Even right now, outside this lodge, it waits." Flashes of Siberia were raw in his mind. "You leave the shelter of this place, I can promise you only death. It lives to eat. So I urge you to calm yourselves, relax, and follow our orders—for your safety."

The crowd looked at Trent with a mixture of fear and outright uncertainty. Was this man with a rifle speaking the truth? Or was this all some elaborately orchestrated ruse at capture?

"What is it?" a voice chanced in the crowd, one of the many voices poking questions.

Trent looked to Heywood, but Heywood was only looking into himself. "An animal. A dangerous, rabid animal."

There were a few laughs, but most looked worried, unsure of what to make about all of this. Soldiers, armed as though ready for battle, ordering folks to keep their calm, informing them that some dangerous sort of animal is waiting outside the lodge, waiting to do bad things to them.

"What sort of animal is it?" another voice asked in concern.

It was right there on his tongue. Shark. That's what it was, a shark. Something that has haunted man on the high blue seas for many long and gibbous moons, stretching back to times unrecorded. The lurking horror beneath the waves. Feared by sailors and buccaneers before the age of machines and iron modernized the world. Further back than records would indicate our species' emergence has man shuddered at that monster with the dead black eyes in the abysmal mysteries of the sea. Even today, the notion of a shark awakens ancient chambers inside the skulls of each. A phantom memory that looks on the sea with trepidation and respect; fearing the King of the cold black gulfs that is the sea. But would Trent admit what truly waited in the snow—what desired the flesh of land walkers?

Before an alternative answer could weave a valid response, automatic weapons fire drew his eyes to the doors.

CHAPTER 16

It was a slaughter. A great and wrathful bloodbath that took no less than several blinks of an eye to complete. A tide of red washed and ate away the ice below it like a pool of acid. No longer was there a scattered ring of bodies, writhing in pain, no longer that single young man dressed for bed.

What had been a desperate attempt at freedom, had come with a fatal consequence. Even with a lack of a moon to radiate the land, barred as it was behind the ceiling of black, the blood shimmered as if hit with a strange luminance.

Lynch had the aspect of one suddenly stricken with a terrible disease, a malady he could not control, the evidence of which beaded down the wall in gloppy trails below the jagged points of the window frame; evidenced on his chin.

Lynch had tried, oh how he had tried to put an end to that threshing beast in the snow. Each bullet that punched into its anemic skin seemed to bounce or deflect as if pinging stone or tungsten steel. Several had found a vulnerable point, burrowing into the hide as claws would rend flesh. Blood, dark and syrupy, pumped from the red dots aside its dorsal. But even as lead entombed its flesh, it continued in its murderous lust.

Lynch watched—helpless and captivated—as the thing chopped and butchered and mutilated and crushed the bones of men and women and children. Its eyes appeared to enhance into two irradiated cores of burning luminosity that scattered away the black with a volatile crimson detonation. Its teeth dripped in ribbons and bands and flaps of flesh and hair, and chips of bone struck into its gums. Blood ornamented its skin red.

"GO TO THE DOOR!" Lynch had shouted—a shout that had found a singular survivor, crawling from beneath a mutilated mass, dragging himself forward with no legs to stand, just a ghastly tracery of what had once carried the man decades of his life.

Lynch put his weapon on the shark after it returned to finish the man. A jerk of the trigger flamed out a stripe of bullets that whistled and punched into its hide, but again, as last time, the rage behind those bullets had no desiring effect.

The shark wriggled and slithered and wormed its way to the fleeting man whose nubs trailed blood and whose screams wedged open the storm. The man, an elderly man of many years, reached into the black sky as snow-frosted his hairy face and brushed past his lips.

Lynch screamed.

Its cavern of teeth separated, drawing the man into its blood-stained maw, falling over him with repeating crunching claps until blood and skin drooled down its wide conical muzzle.

"YOU SONOFABITCH!" Lynch emptied his rifle into the shark. Bullets winged and whined, and for one auspicious moment after a single round had put a gash in its skull, did it seem to reel at the invasive feel of the lead nub planted so close to its mind.

"You don't like that, do you!" he shouted down at the shark. And like a serpent threatened, it slithered through the slime and mutilated remains, seeking its solitude in the snow.

Then Lynch saw something move in that pile of death below. At first, he misinterpreted the subtle shivering of blood and meat to be some pocket of gas released, but after a moment, his clarity improved as a boy—perhaps ten, eleven years of age—emerged from the ring of slaughter. Even at this high angle, Lynch could see the wounded pain present in his eyes.

"UP HERE!" Lynch shouted down to the boy.

The boy looked up towards the voice, saw the man, saw the big chunky flakes veiling a face of concern.

"GO TO THE DOOR! GET INSIDE! NOW!"

Some aberrant strength carried the boy, assisting his flight on legs that quivered as if broken. Only a few yards separated him from the block of light that looked into the grand foyer, a place of safety—a refuge from the beast. He grunted and whined and screamed as he hurried to that beacon of hope.

A shadowy bulk blotted the glass panel set into the door.

The door swung wide, its accompanying warm wave ramming into the boy, and a man stood there, dressed similarly to the one who had shouted at the young man from above.

Relieved, he reached a shaking hand forward, but then exploded in a dreadful scream.

"NOOO!" Trent shouted in the boy's face which had become an agonized death mask. The shark clamped onto the boy just as he reached inside. His body was flung back in the giant maw, feet kicking and arms flailing, blood flooding past its bottom teeth. Both eyes rolled over, seeming to become more charged with the blood coursing down its throat.

Trent put his rifle on the shark, the bolt hammered primer and discharged a wall of burning flame and lead to gash fist-sized holes into the slope of its head. But its effect was a slap on the wrist, a simple warning lacking any real damage.

Immune, the shark macerated the boy into lumps and syrupy tumescent fragments.

Quickly, Trent sealed the door, shutting out the screams and tears and cries for mother and father as the boy bashed his fists on the cone of that murderous monster; ground and sucked down that yawning black throat to liquefy in a bowl of acidic waste.

With his back turned to the outside, Trent looked at the crowd, the air exhausted from his lungs, rifle shaking in one hand.

Out across the large and mostly shocked gathering, a collective horror was seized.

"What—what was that?" a stammering voice asked.

Trent put his eyes on Heywood and saw he had become a mute, lost in a veritable cyclone of thought.

"A shark."

Finally, it had been liberated. A burden released, left to congest minds with wonder and fear and unbelief.

Sounds and shouts and the hammering of thick-soled boots beat down the stairs leading down into the foyer, drawing the eyes of many.

Lynch, Webber, and Baxter ran down those stairs as if chased and hunted by some tremendous beast close and suffocating at their heels.

The men paused.

Saw Trent.

"Did he—" Lynch asked.

Trent nodded. "Dead."

It was at the closing of that single word, like a terrible omen directing doom to the guests, that the sky overhead opened up in a brilliant flash what, remained a mystery, one that would soon be revealed to Alex and his family in the imminent future.

As the storm lashed over the lodge, replacing the heavy biting snow with beads and balls of hail, lightning striking in strange blue belts, Alex cautiously opened the door to his room, when his heart leaped at the sudden loss of lighting that ran down the corridor.

Megan squealed in her throat as the room was swallowed by black. Corrina comforted her, wrapping Megan in her arms, soothing her. Caleb nestled beside his mother, afraid to admit that he was terrified. After all, he was fourteen now, a man in his own eyes. How could a man be afraid of the dark? But it was not the dark that he feared, but whatever drove that man out in the corridor earlier to a raving madness, and those strange and awful screams he caught rising from outside the lodge as the weapon became silent.

"Can't see anything," Alex said, peering out the slant. "Don't think anybody is out there though."

He eased the door back, and carefully stuck his head out into the dark emptiness of the corridor.

"Sweetheart," Corrina whispered—a frightened whisper that snapped out of her. "I don't think you should go out there—just stay with us, we'll be safe in here."

But Alex had to go out there. It was a gnawing sense of curiosity that carried him forward.

"Just taking a quick look," he said.

Softly, he stepped out into the corridor, a snap of lightning tossed a blue sheet on the walls.

Caleb reached forward, an involuntary action he shrank at, careful to avoid showing his vulnerability. "Careful dad."

Alex looked back into the room, back to his family. "Watch over your mother and sister," he told the shadows in the room. "I won't be long."

Into the corridor, with the door sealed behind him, he padded with the lightness of feline paws, flush with the wall. Another flash of blue brought an immediate awareness to him. Up and down the hall, several doors were wide open, only a few remained secure in the frames. He moved carefully toward the window, and could hear sobbing coming from within a room to his left; could hear the hail rattling and smacking vehicle and rooftop, the sound of the earth groaning with thunder following the blue bolts. A wind of ozone and cold blew into his face as he came closer to that shattered window.

Another flash, another wash of blue down the hall. In the brief flicker, Alex saw the pile of brass bullet casings on the floor below the window, sprinkled amidst shards and slivers of glass. A thin layer of snow had dusted the evergreen color of the carpet; squishing beneath his soles.

Alex chanced a look outside the window. From his vantage above, he could see over the parking lot; see the pines waving and shivering as hail and rain struck the limbs.

He looked below the moment an angry fork of lightning drew the shadows away in a blue flash.

Blood caught his eyes, and held it there as the night again swallowed over the human wreckage. In the flicker of light, he saw what looked to be a wide pool of oil, but Alex knew what it was: the evidence of those who had attempted to escape the window, broken down into mulched piles, and scattered inside a ring of crimson.

He stumbled away as if the wind was pushed from his lungs, catching himself on the wall from collapsing. He wallowed back to the room, abandoning his caution, and banged on the door in a fit of fright.

"BABE—IT'S ME—OPEN THE DOOR!"

Corrina swung open the door an instant later.

Alex fell into her as if shoved from behind. Both collapsed onto the ground.

"Oh, god, babe, it's horrible. Those poor—"

With her eyes better adjusted to the dark, Corrina could see the fear on her husband's face. "What is it?" she asked, afraid something had happened to him out in the corridor. "What's wrong, sweetheart? Are you okay?"

Alex choked on his words. "Outside—awful—just awful."

Megan shrieked for her mommy.

Caleb pointed to the door. "Mom, dad, behind you!"

Alex turned, a flashlight beam popped in his face.

Megan screamed.

Caleb screamed.

Corrina dashed over to her children, shielding them behind her.

Alex, blinded by the light, shot up on his feet, and put his hands over his eyes. "Please don't hurt us!"

"Sir, my name is sheriff Robbins, Orris Robbins —I'm the law around these parts. If you could, would you kindly follow me downstairs? We're gathering the remaining guests down below."

"Sheriff?" Alex asked, perplexed.

"That's right, the man who was up here before is downstairs now. He's an American soldier. They ain't here to harm nobody. Now, would you please follow me downstairs?"

Alex looked back to his family as the lodge groaned from thunder. He looked back to the sheriff. "Mind if we get dressed?"

Robbins put his light on the family. "Make it quick."

CHAPTER 18

Jocelyn told him not to worry about it. That the sheriff knew what he was doing up on that mountain; was nothing new up in those undulating hills that he hadn't dealt with before. But the encroaching black, wild storm boiling in the skies, was looking a bit nasty, if not outright dangerous. Jocelyn was a good dispatch, but a bit slow in the head at times. All that faith she put in the man clouded reason. Deputy Douglas Kepler was a man of logic. Earlier, Robbins said he was confronting a group of armed men up at Pikes Trail Head; said he would need reinforcement on the situation. Kepler, good deputy as he was, started up that mountain. A quarter of the way up, Robbins reported that all was secure. Told the deputy that the men were a group of hunters, lost and turned around—said he would be going up to the lodge, check on things there, would be back around nightfall or so—told him not to worry himself and to keep patrolling locally—back in town.

But Kepler worried. Robbins was a man by the

book. Reported each movement and shit and piss that carried him out of his rig. Not a word since that last, Kepler was growing anxious.

He instructed Jocelyn to reach out to the sheriff, but, several attempts later, nothing but dead air—something that Kepler was fearing.

Kepler rang the front counter of White Cap, perhaps they could shed a little light on the matter. But, like the radio, nothing—just a whole lot of rings.

Concerned, Kepler told Jocelyn that he was heading up the mountain, told her to ring deputy Miller, bring him into the station, and forward him any emergency that may arise in the area so he could check on Robbins without trouble. A moment later, his tail lights were two dim points, winding up the Forest Road Four.

Deputy Douglas Kepler wedged his rig through a drift that buried most of the road, a flat slab of white tethered with the woods. What had been familiar before, was an alien place. A place of rising, sculpted ramparts, disgorging from woods that had the look of looming black walls at this late night hours. His headlights punched through the night, clogged with swirling flakes…and rain?

"Damn, looks like one of those freak storms is hitting again. Not good."

He put some more gas into the engine, careful to keep his eye alert to any drops that could indicate a slope.

On his left was Pikes Trail Head, he saw that its security bar was secured, shutting out any curious visitors. But figured with all the snow rising and concealing most of everything, there was no need. Already the snow had all but risen to the surface of the security bar. He thought about throwing his spotlight into the lot, but figured there was no reason to be doing so, instead, he continued up the hill.

Swinging into the driveway, Kepler brought the truck to a halt; rain and hail flicked at his windshield, but even as the sky decided it would obscure his vision with all that witchery above, he saw White Cap, looming mighty and shadowy out there, a host of lumps sitting before it that could only be vehicles, buried with snow and glazed with pebbles of ice.

"Would you look at that."

Blue veins clawed through the black sky, jagged bolts whipped into the woods, and thunder groaned out of the hills, and shook the ground beneath him.

Instantly, Kepler thought back to his childhood.

Scooby-Doo, yep, that's what that big lodge reminded him so much about. The opening scene, with the mansion, creepy and veiled in shadow, fingers of fog rolling past its walls, bats screeching across the screen, and a couple of windows glowing with a yellow light. But White Cap had no light—and no bats. It was a bold structure hit with rain and hail, snow hugging its walls, heavy and thick on its roof; icicles, long pointed like the fangs of some hideous snow beast, dripped off eaves and window frames, ran along the bumper of car, truck, and van.

"Power must be out. Folks are probably losing it about now."

Slowly he eased into the lot, headlights screened in flakes. Instantly, his foot dropped onto the brake; the rig caught some ice and slid a good way before coming to a stop.

"Jesus, God—what the hell?"

His headlights hit it and showed him what he thought he saw to begin with: Blood.

Kepler looked on that massacre a moment, his mind coming up with an answer it was having trouble issuing. Grabbing the handset on the dashboard, he thumbed the mic, "Jocelyn! Get some help out here, there's something wrong. There's blood, Jocelyn—send help! NOW!"

He paused, looking at that red mess, flakes, and hail pinging it, waiting for Jocelyn to key him back.

"Jocelyn!"

Shit, must be the damn weather, he thought, dropping the handset. He grabbed his hat, grabbed his torch, swung open the door, and stepped outside into the cold and streaks of rain.

Flashlight in hand, pistol out, he marched through the snow, the beam of his light bouncing over the ice, hail threading its cone. He stopped not two paces from that glittering ruin of bodies and blood.

"What in God—"

"Kepler!"

It was sheriff Robbins, he'd recognize that voice anywhere.

"KEPLER!"

Kepler put his light on the lodge, saw Robbins face poking outside the door. It looked gaunt and stressed. His hands were cupped around his mouth. "Sheriff? What the hell happened—"

"GET OVER HERE—NOW!"

Figuring with the way Robbins voice was sounding, Kepler avoided the mess, careful not to slide and fall as he moved alongside that tide of red.

He put his light on the sheriff. "Bodies, sheriff, it's awful! What—"

"RUN!" Robbins cut him off.

Kepler stiffened, his face scrunching up. Looking confused, he asked the sheriff, "Run?"

"BEHIND YOU!" No explanation would be adequate, so instead, Robbins had that big pistol of his out. It boomed in his fist, its report echoing across the lot, swallowed by the woods. A single heavy slug drilled a hole in the weather, whistling past Kepler, burying itself in something wet.

Kepler turned, in shock at the sudden crack of that pistol; the smell of its cordite competing with ozone in the air.

"What the shit!" Kepler put his piece—a .357 Smith—on the thing coming at him in the snow. The iron came alive, jumping in his gloved ball of a fist—all six cylinders emptied with the quick stress of nerves blowing off end. He leaped aside, nearly striking his head on the ice-encased bumper of a pickup truck, as something large and streaking with speed, zeroed into him like some sort of white missile with a glowing red warhead for eyes. Something slashed his gut like a blade as the blur of the thing slipped into the night. Blood unzipped from his waist; dumped out of his bowels like water.

"GET TO THE TRUCK, KEPLER! HURRY DEPUTY!" Robbins urged his deputy, scanning the lot with his eyes over that pistol.

Kepler dropped his gun to the ice, the pain causing him to put both hands on his gut, leaving behind his flashlight in the snow. Bowed over, he staggered over to the rig, blood running down the fabric of his tan jeans. Reaching out, he yanked open the door, jumped inside, and quickly swung the door closed behind him.

He looked at the black of his gloves and saw it smeared in thick whorls of blood. A flash of lightning hit the lot.

"God—damn it hurts."

He leaned forward to get a look at the damage to his gut, but couldn't see much in the dark. Snapping on the dome light overhead, he looked again. His blouse had been cut through as if hit with a serrated blade. Past the torn fibers stained red, threaded with bits of tissue, he screamed in fear and pain when he got a look at the big grinning mouth of pink that gashed in his belly, spitting a wave of blood down his legs. In that instant, the flash of what he had seen jumped into his head—momentarily causing a lapse in the pain that was crippling him.

"The fuck was that thing..." He said between clenched and foaming teeth. He turned to the window and saw nothing but rain and hail falling, icing the windshield on his rig. A sharp pain in his gut brought a grunt up his throat. "Damn, I need something to seal this up."

He thought of the aid kit but reaching presented a whole load of challenges he could not face right then. Placed in the back of his rig, the only thing he could do was leave the truck, walk around out back—outside, where that thing was waiting for him. Thinking of that thing, he had to wonder, just what it was he saw. He fought at the absurd image of what he had seen. It couldn't be that—couldn't be what he thought it was. That was impossible.

Probably some rabid wolf, he thought. Some were known to have white fur. The red eyes were probably due to this weather somehow.

Kepler ran through a mental list of critters and meat eaters known to inhabit these woods, but couldn't put a legitimate check mark on any one of them. He wanted to say it—say what it was he thought he saw, because it looked like one

—boy it sure looked like one. But...again, that was highly improbable—something a child would scream about springing up in a dream covered in sweat after watching one of those spooky movies.

Go on, say it.

"A shark." He laughed in his throat—a laugh punctuated with pain. "No—wasn't a shark, just the storm—my nerves showing me things that aren't real."

Something hit the truck.

"What—"

Did it again. Something just below the rig, moving around down there as if it were probing for a weakness. Even as hail continued to hit and thunder grumbled like a hungry stomach, he knew it was thinking of a way to get inside that big metal frame.

Left without his piece, he fumbled at the lock on the .12 gauge mounted beside him. Freeing it, he brought up its eighteen-inch barrel, popped the safety off, and held it awkwardly to his chest, his other hand keeping pressure on the pain picking at his guts like the tip of a good blade.

"The fuck is that..." Something outside, moving along the bumper of a car. It was hard to see much of anything in the dark, especially with all that rain sparking off the ice. He went to narrow his eyes, hoping to get a better bead on the object. But not a moment after his lids sank and became glassy slits, something big was filling the window, shimmering slick from a flash of blue that swept away the night. And leading it through the air were bulbs charged like sun-lanced rubies.

"SHIT!"

It hit the rig with the power of a wrecking ball. Its conical nose was a driving sledge that busted out the driver-side window into a thousand small fragments that cut with the precision wielded of a mob, slashing with razors. Kepler's face suffered, and beads of blood streaked his cheeks and chin, and forehead. Slivers stuck out from his flesh like silver thorns.

He screamed, brought the shotgun up, blew off a shell in the sky, racking another round into the chamber, forgetting the pain leaking out of his belly.

Going to his back, staying low to avoid another thrust of that big white muzzle, he held on to the shotgun, its barrel pointed into the black square of the shattered window. Hail and rain sprinkled through its jagged aperture, pecking at his boots and shin and knees. A shiver ran through him. Lightning flashed.

He swallowed.

A strange scratching noise below the rig caused him to sit up and put his attention on the sound. But the effort, quick as it was, caused him to grunt out in pain, curled over as blood squished out of his gut. "Damnit, losing a lot of blood here..."

Something banged into the bottom.

"SHIT!" the sound caused his heart to leap up his throat.

Suddenly, the truck was hit by what sounded like a dozen pissed-off drunks beating over the frame with hammers and clubs. Kepler swung back down on his spine, his eyes jumping to every window inside the big Bronco, but nothing was there, just bits and bands of ice. After he felt he could take no more of all that noise, it stopped, replaced with a heavy, and pained silence.

As he waited, his heart was the only sound above the rain and hail. It was beating with the imminent feel that it would soon explode.

Then it happened.

The passenger door was hit with a gale of pressure, buckling the door from its frame, tearing it from its housing where it dropped out into the cold whipping sheets of ice.

A scream came rolling up out of his throat as if made by a hundred wailing spirits. This time he saw it. He saw what his mind had wanted him to initially see. It was no white wolf with flaming red eyes. It was a shark. A long and bulky column of meat with a snapping maw that clashed like blades on some distant battlefield.

Frozen by immobility, Kepler could only scream at the sight of those sharp and edged spikes, something that must have been honed on anvils and blacksmith hands.

Snapping from the entrance of its hideous eyes and hungry teeth, he worked the shotgun onto that monster, but was countered as its bulk filled the truck; its massive girth crushing over him.

The smell of meat and blood blew up his nose as those shearing blades chopped the air a foot from his face. It fought to get at him, but found not an inch to squeeze, as though it were stuck.

Using the opportunity to wriggle his gun loose, Kepler got a hold of it, tried to work its blue barrel into that snapping jaw.

"YOU WANT ME YOU SONOFABITCH!"

A grin spread his lips open as the barrel slotted a flapping gill.

The shark thrashed its body at the invasive feel.

"YOU DON'T LIKE THAT, DON'T YOU!"

With his finger firmly on the trigger, he shouted: "CHEW ON THIS YOU BASTARD!"

The gun exploded, but at the last instant that shell broke open, disgorging its pellets into the beast, the shark buckled forward, knocking the barrel loose, swinging it back down towards the deputy.

Kepler screamed wide as a wad of lead balls punched through his face, detonating most of his skull, spraying a clot of bone and brain on the ceiling, leaving him limp and percolating blood from where only a lower ridge of jaw remained.

After the blast, the shark worked its weight backward, aware of the cold, leaking body of meat no longer struggling below it.

Outside the rig, it drew Kepler into its mouth, dragging the corpse into a maw of pink stained teeth where a rapacious chomping of its jaw ground the bones into a pulpy slime of marrow, hacked flesh to strips, and drank down volumes of blood.

CHAPTER 19

Robbins about had himself a heart attack. Maybe a stroke.

He watched, a helpless old fool who had failed to respond to Kepler's screams. But what could he do? Run outside, face the shark? He knew he wouldn't last but a moment outside with that thing out there. It would easily cripple him, chop him down into so many lumps. But the soldiers had enough firepower to obliterate that big mean hunter, but they stood by, watching as he was. Maybe they figured it was useless to attack. Like Chris, they tried to put an end to his misery back out in the lot, but it was far too late. And the bullets that did drive holes into its body, had no real effect—like flies buzzing the tail end of a hog.

"I'm sorry," Trent said, putting a hand on Robbins shoulder.

Robbins turned, wiped a tear out of his eye. "All my fault—should have run outside, did something."

"Nothing you could have done, sheriff," Trent told him. "None of us could have done a damn thing."

Robbins nodded. "Kepler was a good man. An honest man—rare in these times."

"I'm killing that thing," Lynch said, staring out the window into the storm, his hands, hate in his words. "I'm fuckin' killing that monster."

Webber stood beside him. "We'll kill it. That thing is as good as fried and diced and ready to serve with a side of tartar sauce."

Baxter slapped the bolt forward on his MP5, "Just say the word."

Once they had gathered the folks down into the foyer, they had planned to admit what was out there, or at least a variation of such. Admitting there was a shark in the snow, was almost too hard for the mind to announce without a smile or a laugh behind it. Because it was lunacy. That's all it was. Pure insanity. Who would believe there was a shark in the snow? Maybe the children, depending on their age—and there were several young faces looking on the soldiers and the colonel and the sheriff as if they were the scariest men they had ever seen in their young lives. Telling those little, scared eyes, that a shark was hunting men in the snow, would probably not be the best of things to be explaining. Instead, they had come up with some bogus alternative. They would tell the folks that there was a dangerous group of animals outside, ravenous and rabid. Go into details about how they hurt a few folks, and that all the people had to remain indoors until help could arrive to pull them out safely. They were going to tell the crowd, that come daylight, they would gather enough able-bodied individuals to assist in hunting down the wild beasts. It was a far-fetched, half-ass story, that most of the guests would find a bit fantastic to believe, fearing something worse was out in those deep and umbral shadows. But, all of that quick planning came to an immediate standstill once a good percentage of the guests got a look at that monster in the snow, eating that poor deputy outside his truck. The crowd had become silent and withdrawn after that horror. Kids huddled with mommy and daddy, friends comforted one another, it was a quiet calm—a frightened silence.

"I won't allow you to kill it," Colonel Heywood said suddenly.

Trent turned to the man. Saw that look of madness back in his eyes. "Do you intend to stop us?"

Heywood laughed. "I don't need to stop you, sergeant. The moment you step outside, you're as good as meat."

"Who said we would go outside to kill it?" Baxter said, eyeballing the colonel. "We can easily lay it out from inside here—upstairs where we can get a good line on it."

"You think it will just present itself, that it?" Heywood asked. "Do you believe it will allow you to bring it down? I have raised that thing for years now. I have created the perfect machine

—a machine of flesh, designed to eat and kill and think. It is not a simple fish, sergeant, it is a cognizant predator, capable of great feats and countering pathetic human attempts to bring harm to it."

Webber stomped forward, his boots beating away the sound of thunder. His fists balled into knots of steel. "Listen here, Heywood, you may have designed that thing; put your damn heart into that monster, but ain't no man nor beast capable of besting us. We're killing that thing, and I think you know that. So this little tantrum you're throwing is empty air. I strongly suggest you ease up before I restrain you."

Heywood looked at the looming tall man, his dark face chiseled with hate, resembling the wicked contours of a totem demon. "No need to become unglued, sergeant, I'm only warning you."

"And I'm warning you, colonel."

Trent didn't bother intervening. Figured the colonel could piss his pants a bit as Webber laid into him.

Trent stared out into the cold black night, looking at the blood of the slaughter in the lot, glittering over with a pond of ice.

"What are we gonna do, Trent," Baxter asked, putting his own eyes on the red pool.

Trent shook his head. "Haven't thought that far. But I know one thing, we have to act and fast. Make sure the people get some food and rest. We have a long night ahead of us while we work this thing out."

Baxter nodded. "On it."

As Trent kept his eyes outside, he wondered how he would lure that thing to him. How they would snare its attention, just enough, to empty every goddamn bullet they had to give. But like most else that cursed their fates, a cruel and malicious destiny drove a bolt from the sky, striking the needle-like spire rising from the roof —the one Caleb had pointed out the moment he stood beside his father—gashing out a fount of flame and embers that would soon eat up the interior as quick as gasoline poured on a wildfire.

CHAPTER 20

People lost their minds the moment that bolt struck the lodge like a meteor, burning a path that was quickly gutting the upstairs wings with flames. And those dancing orange flames were moving around up there, crawling through each room, breaking everything down in its path like strips of kindling, sweeping down long corridors, bubbling the paint on walls, determined to increase its power, amplify its range.

People were clustered, grabbing at one another as if the mob would provide safety and support to their clutching fingers. But each face out in that blob of uncertainty was scrunched and pained, fearing those hungry flames licking out of that ceiling, eager to boil the flesh from their bones, leaving their skeletons burning and black, a mass of ashes lost to the inevitable sinking of the lodge under a massive pyre.

Alex had hold of his family, piled against him in a wide shaking embrace.

Caleb was a trembling little boy again, much

like the first time he had watched a scary movie one Halloween night. Alex told him it was best he not watch, and to head up to bed, but he was insistent that he wouldn't be scared. Said it would be fun to watch one. Alex agreed, letting him stay up to catch the flick. It was a lesser-known picture, something Alex had found bunched on a shelf in the horror section. The title: NightEaters. It was about a group of strange nocturnal monsters that clawed their way through the floorboards of homes, stealing kids, eating babies, drinking blood from skulls, all that good and wholesome devilry that makes monsters feared and unique to the horror world. Caleb was a ghost after watching those things eat little kids into dripping red ribbons; gnawing on bones that his father told him were probably just wood made to look like bones —or some sort of synthetic creation by the studio. But Caleb believed those were human bones, and it scarred his young mind something nasty. And right then, shivering in his father's arms, he was that little boy again, watching monsters eat babies and drink blood and chew on bones, only a whole lot worse.

Megan was screaming. Screaming as only a little girl is capable in moments of agonizing terror. Her face was a sheet of wet tears, her eyes on the ceiling

"Mommy, I don't want to burn!"

Corrina held her daughter as she once held her as a baby. Soothed her hair with a slap of her hand. "It's okay, sweetheart, we're getting out of this."

But Corrina wasn't sure if she believed they would find an exit out of this horror. She had found her will was shriveling, almost as if she were preparing for death. But still, something in her fought to retain her motherly love for her children—the untamed beauty of a woman strong and mighty in the face of her progenies' impending doom.

Alex racked his mind on a solution that offered no hope. There was nothing positive, nothing but a danger to either approach. They could all sit inside and hope the flames would wither beneath the storm crashing outside, or they chance the snow—chance becoming feed for the thing waiting in it.

Alex had not seen the thing in the snow, but several voices rose in a frightful staccato. Some were saying 'Shark!' He almost laughed at first, but as more and more kept repeating the same word, some in complete delusion about what they were seeing, he had to wonder if they were speaking the truth.

But a shark? In the snow? Such a preposterous thing to scream—especially on top of a mountain —on land! Sharks weren't a species of forest life. They roamed the great seas, swimming beneath the green chop. Perhaps something similarly shaped—a similar symmetry to the hunter of the deep. But again, even that was a bit rough to believe.

As he pondered what to do, gaping black holes opened in the ceiling, tongues of flame shot through, stabbing below, looking for tinder—for flesh.

"We have to get these people out of here—right now!" Webber demanded. "They'll burn—we'll all burn in here!"

Normally a decisive man, Trent had found he had run into the old proverbial wall of thought. There was no reasonable approach to this without dreadful consequences. His initial suggestion would be to head outside, break into vehicles, and seek refuge from the fire. But then he remembered what happened to the deputy; how that shark broke up his truck like a plastic toy. Another idea came in the form of folks waiting it out on top of the tallest truck or van they could find but saw that shark leap a good height, so again, that plan was dashed. Not a whole lot of options were presented at that dire moment. He looked over the crowd—at all the faces, at all the hunched and crouched bodies lowering to the ground, fearing the heat and flames and its increasing speed.

Heywood was rather enjoying this hysteria. Wasn't so much the mania of the crowd as it was that he knew his shark would soon feed. He was scared, yes, Heywood was very scared, much more than he had even been—because he knew what that shark was capable of. But these people, they would be simple feed; sprinkles over a fish tank to be consumed. But Heywood would not become one of those tiny flakes, no. He would find a way out of this, even if people had to die for him to escape.

CHAPTER 21

Flames now spread their tips over the ceiling, and lightning cracked and shook the earth with violent tremors. Hail poured and rain lashed and added ice to the cold blowing across the mountain. But no matter the drive of the storm, its ceaseless curtain of beads and knobs of ice would not come between the flames and inferno chewing through the lodge, consuming down every beam and column that held it for a hundred years.

Faced with the terrible doom of a collapsing burning dome above, the oxygen thinning, the people had decided: they would chance what waited in the snow rather than die and slowly allow the flames to cook them alive.

A massive chunk of the crowd streamed out of the building in a chaotic flash of limbs and screams—a mad, incoherent hive, determined for safety.

Trent and his men were taken by surprise by the mindless mob, overwhelmed by the crowd's unyielding will to live; the fighting spirit that faced death and fought to remove itself from that black doom by any means available.

Deep into the lot, the people gaped into a sky that mocked their efforts at escape, unleashing a torrential wash of ice and stripes of lightning to sheath the white woods, threatening death by mad blue bolts. The earth shuddered beneath as if the claws of titanic monsters scraped the sediment and soil below.

Each footfall out in that polar waste brought misery and terror—dashing hope at the stab of another bolt.

Some curled onto the ground, terrified and shaken by the celestial war in the sky and the thought of that demon lurking near. Others continued into the cold night, putting distance between themselves and the lodge, seeking shelter from both the sky and the jaws of a red-eyed demon.

"What the fuck do we do?" Lynch asked, nearly following the dozens of horror-struck guests outside the door, held back only by the quick restraint of a strong hand.

"Don't even think about it," Trent told him. "One man—not even four well-armed men—could help those people out there. There's nothing we can do for them."

"Fuck!" Webber shouted, the sight of countless bobbing figures deepening through the lot. A trail of flame pissed an arc down the staircase to their backs. A wall of heat pushed into the remaining guests, of which there were only a fraction of what had once inhabited the lodge. "What do we do Trent?"

It was the screams that choked his words away.

Distant screams, far removed from the flames of the burning inferno above. And these were not the screams that were common with fear, even death impending, but of an ancestral awakening of the night and its haunting aspects. It was the cry of ancients faced with towering multi-limbed monstrosities, ravening in blood lust to those seeking escape from its bone-crunching jaws.

Held in a flash of blue, Trent, Webber, Lynch, Baxter, Robbins—even Heywood—were witness to an unspeakable, ghastly slaughter.

Shadowy screaming figures were pulled apart under guttural throat bubbling shrieks that only a body torn of chords could project. It ate through the crowd of distant bold shapes like a swarm of Mako butchering a school of tuna. A flash drew the curtain of night away. What was held in that blue screen was a frosted nightmare. In phenomenal time, the shark had gored the bodies of dozens, leaving only a small element in retreat, back to the lodge of certain death.

A lone man ran with a trail of screams scratching from his throat. But the shark had found his scent—the scent of fear. It drove itself through the lot as if it were back beneath the blue waves, chasing an evading seal. The man, dubious of where to turn, was suddenly struck with a whipping lash of the shark's tail. Its effect was that of a hatchet, cleaving the head from the man's neck which surged with a propulsive fountain of blood behind it, sending the shocked eyes and silent scream high into the hail and rain.

Determined to carry her weight as if she had none to burden her swinging legs, a heavy woman, plump and winded, sought the eternal flames. But, like the man behind her, was hit by a tail that filleted open her waist, allowing a gushing dump of blood and clotted curds of yellow fat to hiss against the nice.

A young couple off to the mother's side fell to gut-squeezing screams, but it did nothing to slow her race back to the lodge, both her children howling in terror at her side. With the shark snapping close behind, the mother lifted her children onto the roof of a hail-encased sedan. As her children scrambled to the center of the roof, the mother slipped on a silky patch below, causing her to stumble. It was then that both children screamed down at their mother with reaching hands. The mighty maw framed the mother, clamping down, folding her into a spongy splash of streaking red jets that painted her children with blood. One kid fell forward, striking his head onto the iced pave, where he lay motionless. He was soon battered between rows of flesh ribboned spikes, unaware of pain the child would never feel. The second child curled into a ball, but his effort at becoming small and an issue to reach proved useless as the shark launched itself from the ground, clamping onto the small figure, punishing his bones under a mouthful of teeth stained with his families blood.

Soon, the lot was a desolate bone land of red waste. Not a single figure was left to stand or hobble on wounds. None survived the shark and its frenzied massacre.

And inside the lodge, the small group of guests that had remained behind looked on over that white field stained with the blood of the slaughtered, enhanced to a blue brilliance thrown by a thrashing storm with no end.

Alex had become an ashen thing. A face no longer holding hope, but shrunken and pitted with black rings etched beneath eyes of two pinpoints inked with trauma. He knew of only one way to free themselves from this nightmare, but its path was riddled with danger.

"The slope," he whispered to himself.

"What sweetheart?"

"The lift on the slope. That's our only hope. It has to work—"

"But the power, sweetheart, there is no power."

"To this building, yes, but those lifts work on their own network. I've seen it on—never mind. That's our only option."

As he discussed this plan with his wife in haste, his words fell not on silent ears. His voice was high and stressed, and the whole of the survivors heard each word. They gathered around him, murmuring agreement and fear as the fire worked a path slowly towards them.

"Are you certain?" Trent wedged into the crowd.

Alex turned to look at the commando. "Yes, I've watched a documentary on skiing and—"

Trent cut him off, his attention back on his soldiers, Robbins, and Heywood—who hadn't turned away from the red sea that was once the lot.

"Let's get these people to the lift."

No words were exchanged, only actions.

The men prodded Heywood ahead of them as the crowd swelled out the back doors leading to the slope.

CHAPTER 22

The men were a silent crescent. The only hint of their presence was the sound of snow crunching beneath their boots. Ahead, tracks punched into the snow leading to the lift, the haggard trail of guests. If screams were rising from their throats, none of the soldiers, nor the sheriff could hear as hail whipped at the trees, sounding much like the snaps of static electricity. Lightning flared blue screens, thunder shook the pines.

As determined as they were to escape the shark, most of the guests were unprepared for the harsh, biting, and clawing gusts streaking over the slope. Some were clothed in no more than sheer lace, frilly nightgowns for bed and play. Still, some had no shirt at all, naked torsos winged with hail and frosted by rain. But others had grabbed their winter protection, bulky coats, or jackets to contain a warmth that was quickly slipping.

Robbins fought to control his legs, finding difficulty to tramp through the snow. He was adamant about keeping pace with the resilient commandos who were a band of bold shadows ahead. Colonel Heywood was struggling a few paces from his side, winded by the exertion.

Robbins thought maybe he should put a bullet in Heywood, save everybody plenty of grief. What would it matter if he fell to a well-placed notch in the skull or to a dripping cave of teeth? He thought about Kepler, dying as he did, screaming and fighting that shark. The memory of his death was urging him to end that army man right there. Would the soldiers mind if he were to exact a little backwoods vengeance? It was hard to say, but he kept his cool about him. At least for the moment.

Heywood stared at the line of commandos ahead, shadowed by the woods. He thought about that Beretta 9mm on his hip—thought about problems that could easily be solved. But surely, killing four men—experts in the craft—would require talents above the simple marksman of a common soldier. He might get lucky, and strike a fatal shot, but would his second, his third, and his fourth be as lucky? The men hand banded together, a unit of traitors, destined to bring his shark—his creation—down. He believed they could, but it would require a supreme effort, one he knew they were capable of. Unfortunately, left without too many options of escape in the meantime, he would have to rely on their shield. But once liberated from their grip, he would make an attempt at their heads.

Somewhere behind the two straggling men, a

scream broke through the night.

Robbins and Heywood turned.

Four limping shadows emerged around a clump of scrub pines, snow up around their knees. What put Robbins eyes wide, were the two red points of light on their tail.

"SHARK!"

Drawing a bead on the shark, Robbins gun leaped as a flame licked out of the barrel, discharging two slugs that slapped into the beast just as it reared out of the snow like some giant slab of earth.

But if it felt anything, it was showing no pain. Its mouth fell open, chopping up a small body that cried out with a heartbreaking scream. A flash of blue hit the scene, revealing a prostrate man, wild with hysteria, falling quick like the first, dashed apart in a feral frenzy. Black plunged over the land, and the only color in that shadow veiled frostscape was the pair of crimson bulbs. Two more screams shrieked in the dark.

Robbins fired blindly; again and again, his hammer striking primer until smacking empty.

"YOU FOOL!" Heywood shouted, slapping at Robbins arms. "YOU'LL KILL IT IF YOU KEEP SHOOTING IT!"

Robbins cuffed Heywood in the lip, putting him on his back in the snow. With shaking hands, he swung open the cylinder on his pistol, dumping out the shells. Plucking a speed loader from his belt, he slammed home a fresh load of .44 caliber ball lead. A quick jerk of his hand, the cylinder locked back into place. He put the barrel on the colonel and drew the hammer back.

"Give me one reason not to put one of these in your goddamn head!"

Heywood sat limp in the snow, but a grin slowly spread his lips like a knife opening a throat. "I apologize, sheriff Robbins, for my reaction. You must excuse my abrupt burst of passion. I suppose I just feel a connection with the shark. Much like a mother to her child when there is a danger to its life—"

"SHERIFF—ON YOUR SIX!"

Robbins looked up from the colonel, into the face of Trent.

A sudden loud crack behind him brought his body to twist. The lodge was a burning mountain of flames. Strong beams popped with pressure, disabling the lodge into a ruin of flaming coals. Even as rain and hail attacked the land, it did nothing to abate the effect of the raging fire.

Heywood cackled madly as a band of lightning struck the world blue.

Orris was caught unaware of its approach. Before he could react or dive from its path, it shot towards him with a speed that troubled his eyes. The burning pyre of the lodge accentuated the horror of the shark. Like a frightful image of a beast released from the molten gulfs of hell. Its eyes lighted with absolute lust, its jaw sprung wide as if wound to spring at the last moment, its teeth bunched with bits of flesh, inked in blood.

"I'M SHERIFF AROUND THESE PARTS!" It was the last words that left his shouting lips following a booming report that hammered a single shot to cut into its throat the moment the beast raised out of the snow, a rampart of death, sheathing Robbins down to the boots in a bursting spray of blood.

CHAPTER 23

All notion of escape withered inside Trent as he watched the shark juice Robbins into a pile of gore. Safety was no concern as he raised his rifle on the still feeding shark crunching quarters of Robbins between its ungodly fangs.

It was the initial burst of his rifle that started the mayhem—that started the shark in its advance on the men. Soon, the three remaining soldiers followed, adding their rage to stream from their weapons. Bullets came together in a storm of screaming steel, punching red holes in the skin of the shark as it weaved through the snow.

Lynch had abandoned knowledge of marksmanship and discipline, reverting to a horror-struck lunatic; a knuckle-dragging primate entrusted with the sword of his God. His weapon was a chaotic flash of flame and flinging brass, quaking in his arms as bullets roared and bore open tunneling rents that sprayed black blood. A single bullet stabbed into the vibrant center of its eye, pulping the socket into a running, blistered trail of slime. But still, the shark rushed through the snow, determined to reach the men and their magic wands laying waste to its shell.

Webber and Baxter were a shouldered unification of death.

Each of their weapons drew away the shadows around them so only their aspects were lighted by the flames of muzzle flashes. Their bullets gashed across the thick hide, stitching patterns down its skull; but it seemed no matter how many rounds sought and lanced its skin the thing charged through the snow as if driven by the hands of unseen demons.

Closing fast, its swift propulsion through the snow was a smooth action that could have taken place in the sea. It hungered and it craved, and if it could, it would salivate at the men paces away from its clashing jaw.

Heywood had sought the shield of a frozen pine bole, avoiding the streaking white column of death that tore past him through the snow as a torpedo hurled from the nose of a submarine. He looked on the beast as the ultimate creation —his ultimate creation. The perfect monster; the perfect weapon designed by his hands—only his hands! He watched in a grim amusement— an anticipating smile lining his face as it drove towards the commando team, resistant to their feeble and laughable assault.

Then a scream assailed the night, a piercing agonized shriek.

And Heywood's grin spread wide—wide as the grin painted on a clown.

Lynch flopped on his back, struggling to right himself on legs he no longer possessed, taken by that shark in a terrible flash of its teeth. Both stumps flailed and spit whorls of blood.

But it wasn't finished.

It was circling the men surely as if they were a stranded vessel on a still sea.

Lynch watched as its dorsal sliced through the ice, and he winced at the loss of his rifle. The commandos snapped off erratic bursts that only kicked up the snow behind its path.

Then as he watched the dorsal near, it slipped beneath the snow.

Fearful, he looked around him, at the black woods rising over him. Webber crunched forward to assist in removing Lynch, dragging him back, but as he took not three steps in the thick bed, the shark burst from the pack like a missile launched from a silo.

Lynch screamed as the maw opened below him, macerating his anatomy into a pulped, exsanguinated ruin—carried down into the belly like the tide of a surging river.

Baxter rushed ahead, a fierce wind brushed beside Webber who had been shocked by the immediate death of Lynch.

He ran into the woods where he last saw the dorsal sink into the snow, a trail of red behind it. Blind and his veins running with rage, his death was meaningless as he sought to vindicate the death of his teammate—his brother.

His weapon burped in silenced streaks, smacking pine and kicking snow. A belt of lightning drowned the woods blue.

"SHOW YOURSELF!"

The wait was not long.

As if prepared for the man's fallacy, the shark blew from the snow an ambush. Its tail whipped forward, cleaving Baxter down the center into two perfect slabs that instantly dropped to the snow.

The shark settled itself into the cool and thick bed of the ice, its mouth drawing over each slab, chopping it down into a sludge that eased its volume down its throat.

Thing was, Webber saw the whole thing. And his scream jumped over the woods like that of a lion's powerful roar.

His weapon shook in his hands as he emptied a thirty-round stack into the dark woods, where most of the bullets whacked pine or slotted snow.

"Webber!" It was Trent. He had dashed to his friend's side the moment Baxter was taken in a flash of lightning. "We have to move, there's nothing we can do here!"

"Bullshit!" he snapped back, his eyes inflamed

to terrifying points. "There is one thing I'm doing before I fall to that goddamn shark!"

"Don't be a fool, Webber. That thing is more than we can handle—more than your gun can handle. We put everything into that goddamn thing, and still, it came."

Webber staggered away from Trent, a gesture that caused grief inside of him. "Sorry, brother, but I have to do this—for Baxter—for Lynch." He turned away, facing the woods, back to where that shark had split open Baxter.

"It's not worth it, brother. That thing is too damn strong."

Webber slouched his shoulders and turned to face Trent.

"I ain't after no shark. I figured that thing is either gonna' kill me right now, or allow me life long enough to get what I'm after."

"What are you talking about?"

"My beef is with Heywood—"

Trent nodded.

"I ain't leaving this mountain until I find him. You hear what I'm saying?"

Trent understood exactly what he was saying. He wished the man would rethink what he was intending to do, but how could he convince a man who had watched his own brothers mutilated by something that shouldn't even exist?

"I got you covered, brother," Webber winked. "GO!"

Trent set his jaw tight, eyes wetting over. He

cursed Heywood—cursed the shark—cursed the death that hung as a plague over the land. He cursed the lunacy of the situation. But, he understood, understood only as a brother would ever understand.

"Brick—"

"Go," Webber told him, not bothering to turn a look into his brother's eyes, afraid of what would reflect—knowing that same look was held in his own.

CHAPTER 24

Webber had no compunction for killing a man of his own service. Wouldn't upset him in the slightest. Heywood was essentially a tumor, something to be carved out. And Webber was hoping to get his chance at a bit of carving. If he could just slip up on him like a shadow, he wouldn't have to waste what few bullets he had remaining. He would use that knife on the man. Dig around his throat some until a hot wave ran down his arm.

Crouched low as if moving through enemy territory, which it pretty much was hostile, Webber kept the gun ready. It was hard to tell if the hail was easing up a pinch, or if the trees, bunched together like they were around him, were shielding the fall. Either way, it was good to get out of the teeth of that storm.

Something snapped the moment a blue flash ran through the woods.

Webber stopped, his body tensing.

"Fuck you get to, Heywood," he whispered to

himself.

He stepped forward when another snap brought his gun to the spot. Another crack to his immediate right caused him to jerk a burst into the woods.

"Fuck."

He swept the woods with eyes blacker than the night. Flames jumped and ate what was left of the lodge.

"Looking for me?"

A line of ice went right along Webber's spine. He turned, weapon on Heywood who was standing there like some sort of crazed and mindless thing.

"I figured you would stay behind—a man like you is a loyal soldier. A soldier's soldier! A noble hero to avenge his comrade's death. Is that right?"

Webber kept that suppressor on Heywood as he walked a tight circle.

"Don't you think it's best to at least perhaps try the tranquilizer? Perhaps we could have avoided all this senseless killing. Are you willing to die—"

"Are you?" Webber interrupted the colonel.

"It could have all ended long ago, back in the parking lot where that poor young man was…well, you remember—"

"You're so fuckin' sure that damn needle of yours works," Webber shook his head. "It's useless —just like you."

Heywood laughed. "Useless? I think not, my friend. It has a powerful sedative ready to inject and paralyze. It will work, as long as—"

"Shit don't work," Webber told him. "Know how I know that? Because I pulled that fuckin' pistol out, popped a dart into that thing when it was chewing on Lynch, and it had no fuckin' effect. Our bullets proved more effective."

Heywood again threw back his head with a laugh. "Your bullets might as well be pebbles to my shark, sergeant Webber. And I'll admit, I should have designed the needles to have a more durable thrust. I guess it's back to the drawing board. But… one more thing," Heywood said, an awful, curling grin on his face. "It works fine on human skin."

The silver pistol came up, spit out a single dart that hissed from the muzzle trailing an incandescent mist, slamming into the breast of Webber, who instantly went stiff as a board, dropping the submachine gun to the snow.

On his back, his eyes rolled—the only manipulation allowed of the body.

"See, instant work. Very effective I might add." Heywood grabbed the MP5. "It's also a great poison used to interrogate captives; to arrest those terrible screams that are common to victims under great torture." He lowered the muzzle down to Webber's knee. "Example?" The gun jumped. Webber's eyes rolled in a silent face. "How about another?" Another silenced report of bullets tore across his belly, blood spilled into the snow. "How does that feel, sergeant? I know you can still feel the pain, there's just no way to express it—is there?"

CHAPTER 25

Alex had pushed his family through the dark woods in a relentless path that troubled their shaking bodies. Trailing behind them, were the screams of many—the last screams proceeding death. Weapons fire raged and occasional glimpses of the burning lodge spoked through the tight pines.

"Up here!" Alex pointed to the shadow-framed lift.

Corrina had hold of Megan, who had become a trembling sculpture of fear and ice. She had said nothing since the family evaded the monster in the snow, trudging through the black woods, no light to guide, just the strange and ghostly flickering of flames parting the night in brief beams—the occasional snap of blue.

"Are you sure this will work, sweetheart?" Corrina asked winded by the strain of her muscles and lungs. "What if it doesn't?"

"It will work—it has to!"

Alex hoped it would. The options beyond were limited, if not outright slim to absolutely none. He had one in mind, but it would require effort his family—even himself—had lacked. Strength and perseverance were the keys to this plan. He would guide them up the nearest mountain, the foot of which would tax their already screaming muscles. Surely that thing could not climb a mountain? But the path would be a treacherous one, and the shark could easily intercept them, even now—it could rise out of the earth, take them with one mighty crash of its jaw.

Reaching the summit, the family fought forward, seeking the shelter provided by an open-air structure with a flat roof, dripping long and tapering icicles around its rim. It was designed as a waiting area for skiers; a place of rest before they chanced the slopes again.

Protected from the hail and rain, Alex addressed his family. "This is our only chance. If this doesn't work, we have to get to those mountains. I see no other way for us to get out of this."

Corrina's face dropped. "The mountains? But, there's no—"

"It's our only option if this doesn't work—there's nothing else we can do. If we sit here, we're as good as dead. And I don't want that."

Corrina rocked Megan in her arms.

"Son," he said to Caleb, "I'm going to need your help."

Caleb stood, a look of pride in his eyes, screened behind a mind wracked with terror. "Okay, dad."

Alex pointed and looked at his wife. "That box

over there—that's the auxiliary station. It will power this lift. I want you and Megan to take a seat on that chair right there. Soon as the power is running, your two will be carried away—"

"But what about you and Caleb?" Corrina asked, nearly screaming the question.

Alex moved over to his wife. Planted a long kiss on her lips. Kissed his daughter on the head. "We'll be right behind you—I promise."

Caleb ran up and wrapped his arms around his mother. "I love you, mom."

Tears ran in silver streaks down her face. She couldn't believe this was happening. It was like some nightmare—an endless nightmare, trapped and suffocating. But the cold was real, the threat of death lurked behind each tree, and under the snow at her feet.

She looked into her husband's eyes. "I love you both. Please hurry."

Alex and Caleb busted open the cheap lock securing the flimsy sheet metal door. Inside: the guts of power. There was a black knob jutting aside a bank of switches. He tried the knob, jerking it down.

Nothing happened.

"Must be these switches—have to hit the right ones."

Caleb looked into the woods that loomed high around the shelter. "Hurry dad."

"I'm trying—how's your mother and Megan?"

Caleb looked to the chairlift and saw his mother rocking his sister who still held that stone aspect. "They're fine, dad."

"Wait—" Alex said. "I think I got it."

Another jerk of the knob and the lift hummed with the power of electricity.

"Yes!" Caleb shouted in relief.

"Let's get back to you mother—"

Corrina screamed.

Megan screamed.

Alex dropped to his knees, and Caleb collapsed beside him, spastic and shrieking as a little boy. "MOMMY!"

Before the chair swept forward, the shark had broke open the snow below her feet, dragging Corrina and her daughter into its bullet-butchered maw. Blood burst around its muzzle as it chopped Corrina and Megan down deep into its throat.

Alex ran forward, but his momentum was hampered, paralyzed at the sight of his wife— the sight of his daughter—reduced to waves of sludging red.

"CORRINA!MEGAN!" It was one word, strung viciously and heartbreaking. It was the cry reserved for pain that should never be felt.

Caleb was balled in the snow, shivering and catatonic. No longer did he see, no longer did his tongue respond. But he could hear, and he was hearing the sounds of his mother's and sister's bones snapping like gunshots inside that giant blood-stained maw.

As he crested the incline, he watched in unutterable horror as the thing masticated the family between its teeth. Trent charged forward, shouting and stampeding through the snow, his rifle sharp and harsh. Bullets winged its backside, brass flinging with speed from the port. Left with only a single magazine, he hurried to insert the stack into his empty rifle. Dropping the bolt, he raised his weapon, zeroed on the skull, and jerked out a single shot.

The bullet screamed across the space, crashing into the flesh in an eruption of bone and pink.

Instantly, the shark slipped back beneath the white frosted wave of ice.

Trent dashed through the dark woods as lightning snapped the world blue. He saw the father, the son. His stomach tightened. And even over the horror of the episode—from the wastes of Siberia to the death of his team and so many left in the shark's path—his resolve had wavered only slightly. Right then, he had to keep what little he had left.

He wanted to say he was sorry. That if he and his team were better marksmen, then perhaps the beast would have fallen long ago. But what matter would it make if he dropped to his knees in supplication to a laughing God, or spill his sorrows to this damaged father in the snow aside his son?

"Get on the lift—now!"

Alex looked up into the man's face above him.

There was not much to see if he were even human. "My wife…my daughter—"

"And for the sake of your son, take your boy, get on that lift—now!"

Movement in the pines to his rear dropped Trent into a cat-like crouch. His weapon menaced the shadows that held as ink between each column of frozen pine.

He looked over his shoulder. "Goddamnit, go!" he shouted to Alex.

Alex wondered who this man was. Why his team was here—why there was a shark in the snow —why a mountain of guests now lay dead—mere smears and stains on the ice. But what reason would he have to question things at this time? It was time for him and his son to leave this ground, to get high above it where even the shark would struggle to reach.

Without a word shared, Alex grabbed his son, carried him in his arms, and lumbered through the snow, heading to the lift.

Trent had his eyes on the woods, in one particular spot where he discerned movement. It was faint, but it was there. He wondered if maybe he had killed the shark. But he didn't think so. Even a well-placed shot could not bring such a hunter down. Heywood had said the shark could sustain heavy damage before succumbing to its wounds, and Trent wished at that moment he had brought along grenades, explosives, a LAW rocket, something with a real punch. But there were no such things available, and like any soldier faced with such issues, he could do nothing but carry on, and do what he does best.

Just then, a shadow was revealed by a blue flash. Trent tensed.

A hiss streaked out of the woods, and, call it a finely honed intuition, but Trent ducked the winging projectile before it slammed into him.

"Heywood!" Trent screamed behind a ripping burst of his rifle.

The shadows had enclosed the woods again.

"Come on you sonofabitch! Come out here!"

All around was a natural silence. Only the sound of the sky, the elements at war, but nothing stirred with the signature of human, animal, or beast.

It happened quickly. A singular flash drew away the night, and in that brief blue world, Trent saw Heywood, running towards him in the snow, the silver pistol out ahead of him. The dart whistled from the cylindrical muzzle.

Trent fell to the snow; his rifle dropped beside him.

Heywood stepped forward, the shadows peeling around him, revealing him in a natural glow thrown up by the white snow.

"Oh, Trent, so easily duped. Just another dumb soldier I suppose. But I figured somebody like you would be more aware. I'm a simple scientist, not a commando-like yourself. You would think after years of hunting men and killing our nation's enemies, that you would be something impossible to oppose," Heywood laughed. "But, like any man, you're a victim of your grief. Had your men—and all those people—not died on this mountain, perhaps you would have had the drop on me before I, you."

Trent rolled his eyes in his skull.

"Now that I have you here, I'll show you how I took care of Webber, or...Brick, as you men call him."

Heywood came forward, the Beretta 9mm in his fist. "You see, I let him feel plenty of pain before the shark eventually finished him. It was quite simple really. Such a stupid fool, like all of you. Expendable assets—trash to be discarded and replaced by yet more fools."

Trent could do nothing but roll his eyes, and each rolled in strange circles.

"Speaking of pain, Trent. How would you like to feel a bit before my project finishes you off?" He lowered the pistol over Trent's knee. "Like—"

Trent sat up, a silver pistol in his fist. "You know something, Heywood: you talk too much."

The silver tube jumped in his hand. The dart struck Heywood in the throat. His eyes went wide, locking in place, collapsing to the cold snow.

Grabbing up his rifle, Trent looked down on the colonel. "This is for Lynch—for Baxter—for Brick."

Trent hurried away, back to the lift.

Heywood felt the ground shudder beneath him and knew it was not struck with thunder. His eyes rolled in his skull. Something large broke the surface of the snow, showering him in bits of ice and flakes.

It came beside him. One eye, charged and malefic, looking into his own.

I guess it's time we meet again, Heywood thought. Come and get it, boy.

A single clap of its maw separated Heywood from his torso, leaving a gaping space between head and legs, and a clotted smear spreading red.

Trent saw the man and his boy above the ground in a flash of lightning. They had made the lift, and were safe for now. But the chairs would return to the surface, and Trent had to make a decision. His rifle jumped in his arms as he emptied each bullet into the auxiliary panel. Blue sparks burst and showered the snow. The lift came to an immediate stand-still.

All around and above the mountain, celestial war raged.

On his knees, reflection came to him in fleeting glimpses. A historical line that revealed his past in a billion flashing moments.

And there, looming above him, was that yawning black cave crammed with bullet holes and rows of teeth. He screamed into its throat as it crunched down onto his bones, drawing out his blood and meat in flinging gashes that flared over and down the slope.

CHAPTER 26

"Did you see the headlines?" Secretary Conner asked the general seated across from him, framed by a backdrop of the Potomac spotted in ice.

"Yes, I glanced over them. Saw where it mentioned the massacre at the lodge and the bodies that were counted. One hundred twenty-five, if I'm not mistaken."

"And not a soul suspects it was something... beyond human?"

"That is correct, secretary. It was assumed the men they had found were members of an as-yet known terrorist group; that the armed individuals were responsible for the murder of over a hundred American citizens."

"And what of their records, general?"

General Coy Hall sat forward, his elbows resting on the walnut surface of his desk. "Deleted. There is no record of these men—nothing that will lead back to us or their service with the army. Wiped, sir."

"Very good, general."

"But what of the boy who survived?"

"The Caleb boy?" Hall asked.

Conner nodded.

"He was intercepted on his way to the hospital. He and the ambulance crew were taken care of on a strip of forest road."

"Another job well done." Conner shook his head. "It still is a shame, I suppose. A boy and his father left high on the lift in that cold. The father was frozen solid when they found him, is that correct?"

Hall nodded. "Correct, sir."

"Enough of this dredge, what of the shark?"

"We're keeping a close eye on the shark, I can assure you. The sun will soon cleanse the land of frost, and then it shouldn't be hard to find. Likely will find its way to a lake, or river. Mayhap we'll never know. But its terror will be short-lived in the meantime.

"What's the next step, general?"

"I've ordered production of the shark. Luckily for us, Heywood was much too foolish to lock up his blueprints for the beast. I have men working on it now."

"Excellent. I expect an army of these monsters come next winter."

Hall nodded.

"What's on the agenda for today, Hall?"

The general sat back in his high-back leather chair. "Thought I would get some air, go for a walk later, then find a nice corner in some dusty tavern in Georgetown. Would you like to join me in a celebration?"

"Sounds like a deal. I'll see you tonight." Conner stopped before leaving the office, and turned to face the general. "Oh, and general, excellent work on the operation."

General Hall sat back, swinging his face to the grand window looking out over the storied river. It was a great operation, he thought. And to think, Heywood thought it was a freak occurrence in the avionics of the craft. Such a gullible fool.

Hall threw back his head and laughed loudly.

AFTERWORD

Hope you enjoyed! This is the first in a new series titled: VHS Trash! Just a fun collection of titles that will include all sorts of wild tales. VHS Trash 2 coming August 2022!

Printed in Great Britain
by Amazon